SLEEPLESS NIGHTS AND DAYS OF GLORY

A Novel

ESSENTIAL TRANSLATIONS SERIES 45

Canada Council **Conseil des Arts**
for the Arts **du Canada**

ONTARIO ARTS COUNCIL
CONSEIL DES ARTS DE L'ONTARIO

an Ontario government agency
un organisme du gouvernement de l'Ont

Canada

Guernica Editions Inc. acknowledges the support of
the Canada Council for the Arts and the Ontario Arts Council.
The Ontario Arts Council is an agency of the Government of Ontario.
We acknowledge the financial support of the Government of Canada through the
National Translation Program for Book Publishing, an initiative
of the *Roadmap for Canada's Official Languages 2013-2018:*
Education, Immigration, Communities, for our translation activities.
We acknowledge the financial support of the Government of Canada.
Nous reconnaissons l'appui financier du gouvernement du Canada.

HÉLÈNE RIOUX

Fragments of the World III

SLEEPLESS NIGHTS AND DAYS OF GLORY

Summer Solstice

A Novel

Translated by Jonathan Kaplansky

GUERNICA EDITIONS

TORONTO – BUFFALO – LANCASTER (U.K.)
2019

Original title: *Nuit blanches et jours de gloire* (2011)

Copyright © 2011, Les Éditions XYZ inc.

Translation copyright © 2019 Jonathan Kaplansky and Guernica Editions Inc.

Michael Mirolla, editor

Cover and interior design: Errol F. Richardson

Guernica Editions Inc.

1569 Heritage Way, Oakville, (ON), Canada L6M 2Z7

2250 Military Road, Tonawanda, N.Y. 14150-6000 U.S.A.

www.guernicaeditions.com

Distributors:

University of Toronto Press Distribution,

5201 Dufferin Street, Toronto (ON), Canada M3H 5T8

Gazelle Book Services, White Cross Mills

High Town, Lancaster LA1 4XS U.K.

First edition.

Printed in Canada.

Legal Deposit—Third Quarter

Library of Congress Catalog Card Number: 2018968506

Library and Archives Canada Cataloguing in Publication

Title: Sleepless nights and days of glory : summer solstice : a novel / Hélène Rioux ;
translated by Jonathan Kaplansky.

Other titles: Nuit blanches et jours de gloire. English

Names: Rioux, Hélène, 1949- author. | Kaplansky, Jonathan, 1960- translator.

Series: Essential translations series ; 45. | Rioux, Hélène, 1949- Fragments of the world ; III.

Description: Series statement: Essential translations series ; 45. | Fragments of the world ; III.
| Translation of: Nuit blanches et jours de gloire.

Identifiers: Canadiana (print) 20190045558 | Canadiana (ebook) 20190045620 | ISBN
9781771834674
(softcover) | ISBN 9781771834681 (EPUB) | ISBN 9781771834698 (Kindle)

Classification: LCC PS8585.I46 N8413 2019 | DDC C843/.54—dc23

For Élise

Contents

1

On the Terrace of
the End of the World

*One quarter, perhaps a third, of
humanity lives at night ...*

It is the time that goes by between sunset to sunrise. Night. They say night falls. True, without much of a to-do, it falls but every day, sometimes early, sometimes late, when the sun goes down behind the horizon to emerge on the other side. Because, no matter what they say, it never sets: it's just that we don't see it anymore. So it is with life. Then darkness, little by little, swallows the light. The street lamps come on along the roads, the highways, and lighthouses are illuminated along the coasts. And stars, or the memory of them, their reflection – some apparently have been dead for centuries or even longer – appear as if by magic in the dark sky. Night is here until tomorrow.

Sometimes we say it reigns. But usually we say that when things are going badly in the world, the Dark Ages, the Great Darkness and all that. We would just as soon not see it reign.

Dark, deep. Evil at times. Or we speak of a night of bombings – when a series of terrorist acts is perpetrated. A killer crouching in a corner, a spy wielding sophisticated instruments: Night-time is and will be their accomplice. A sniper lying in wait and his prey who, carrying a briefcase full of top secret documents, millions of real or counterfeit dollars, laundered or not, exits his car, his sailboat, his luxury hotel, suspecting nothing. A bullet goes through his windpipe – or is it his heart? The poor guy collapses in slow motion; in a movie his fall would be almost elegant. A stream of blood on the lawn, the parking lot or perhaps the water of the marina suddenly becomes red. But then you don't see the red at night: Everything is black or grey. The hit man vanishes without a care. Swallowed up like light, he as well, by night-time. No one witnesses the incident – the murder – except for the moon, but she's slipped behind a cloud. In any case, she's seen worse, having contemplated the world since they emerged from nothingness together.

Let's go back in time. In a clearing, we see witches in a trance dancing with Lucifer. Farther on, the pyres roar. But they were perhaps – probably – lit during the day so people could see the sinners squirm and grimace in the flames. A necessary sight for the edification of the masses, all inquisitors agree: Torture should be convincing enough to keep the people docile for a while. The Ku Klux Klan burn theirs, or crosses, at night, as seen in documentaries. Huge crosses that roar with the same vengeful furor as the pyres of time past.

Night: Some people associate it with sin, the dark side of the soul, as well as with silence, fear, and mystery. All kinds of maledictions are attributed to the moon, that eye traveling through the sky, and to her light shimmering on the sea. Curses, and inexplicable, sinister phenomena, especially at full moon, when Count Dracula and his fellow ghouls leave their coffins, the living dead awaken and, driven by malevolent designs, prowl around cemeteries. More babies are born than on other nights, crazy people grow agitated in their cells and must be tied to their beds. The howls echoing down the corridors of the asylum no longer have anything human about them, we're told. Luckily, at dawn, everything goes back to normal. But not always.

Some find it sad. People think of the night that they called, that they still call *La Noche Triste* – the Night of Sorrows. The night of June 30, 1520, when the Spanish, who were surrounded, tried to flee Tenochtitlan, despite the destroyed bridges. It was raining; it rained all night. Torrential rain. Later, if we are to believe the chroniclers – but why wouldn't we? – the conqueror bedecked in steel cried at the foot of a tree after counting his dead warriors, pierced by Aztec spears, or, worse destiny, sacrificed to pagan deities, implacable, drowned at the bottom of the lagoon beneath the weight of the stolen gold. Yes, the great Hernán Cortés cried at the foot of a cypress. *Se le saltaron las lágrimas de los ojos,* says the chronicler, overcome by emotion. Tears well up in his eyes. This tree that in Nahuatl they call *ahuehuete* still exists, apparently, in Tacuba. At least what's left of it. Its son or daughter – do trees have a gender? – a cypress they claim was begotten by it – a seed fallen and germinated in the ground – now watches over the older one.

Nox. Feminine, like the words for light and water in French, like the earth. Scheherazade unveiled who tells the sultan her thousand and one tales, the beautiful Soraya in the Tower of the Captive, in the Alhambra.

In the forest, no – or hardly any – sound. Not in the city, either. Life is dozing. Let it rest. But no, all is not asleep. A quarter, a third perhaps of humanity is awake. Ambulance drivers, fishermen, doctors on call, nurses, taxi drivers, bartenders, disk jockeys, nude dancers – and the people who watch them wiggle their hips. Writers and journalists, policemen, private detectives. Burglars and drug dealers. Hit men. Insomniacs and night owls. Wandering souls. An owl hoots in the woods – it doesn't sleep; it stalks its prey. The sea is calm. In the open sea, three fishing boats appear to be rocking back and forth. The gleam of lighthouse pierces the darkness at regular intervals. Then, out of nowhere, for an instant, you catch a whiff of something that delights the senses. Spellbound, you turn your head. It is Queen of the Night and its scent is bewitching.

Nyx. Daughter of Chaos for the Ancient Greeks. Mother of sleep and dreams, of old age, of destiny. And of Thanatos whom she begot alone, Thanatos with a heart of iron. Death.

They say it's best to sleep on things, that night is the realm of the unconscious, of dreams – as if we didn't dream during the day. In the minds of those sleeping, characters enter and leave, plots are hatched

3

and are not unravelled. Time stretches out, twists around, then unfolds; it no longer means anything. It speaks its own language. In the morning, disconnected images still remain like shards of a shattered mirror.

But white nights conjure up images of wild parties, raves, orgies and other gatherings enlivened with illicit substances. Or lovers who moan, shout, sigh, sweat, embrace in bed, a writer imploring his recalcitrant muse. Run out of inspiration, forehead resting in his hand before the page in front of the page covered in crossings out – or is it a blank screen? Jazz on the radio, cats in heat growling, tomcats challenging each other in the alleyways.

White nights make us think of the north: Iceland, Siberia, Alaska, St. Petersburg, Dostoevsky and his characters – other souls in disarray – continue to wander, forever deprived of sleep. Velchaninov, Pavel Pavlovitch, the eternal and pathetic husband with his crepe-bedecked hat, Nastenka who wanders near a canal, waiting for love – but will love come? And the others, Myshkin, Karamazov, Rogozhin, Nastasya Filipovna: all their heightened torment, all their remorse. *The red moon over the Neva*. A gypsy violin, a guitar, an arrogant dancer with her fringed shawl, a fist on one hip, opposite arm raised above her head. Gold bracelets jangling on her wrists. Vodka and champagne flowing. Laughter and tears. Curses, pledges, betrayals. A little farther on, nihilists, eyes feverish, try to reconstruct the world, or take it apart, in smoky basements around a samovar.

Those basements bring others to mind: Saint-Germain-des-Prés, for instance; the skinny singers dressed in black, hair in their eyes, the disenchanted philosophers, yes, that crowd went out at night, that's for sure, and only came home at dawn. We can still hear the echo of drunken voices, hoarse after holding forth and smoking so much. Visionary poets and painters, inspired choreographers with their star dancers, their ballerinas, depressive novelists like fireflies, their fame long faded. Jean Cocteau and his friends, perhaps. Firebirds, night birds. Expatriates crazy with freedom, the lost generation. They emerge from those basements only to enter others. Some of them totter on their high heels, arms around each other's shoulders. An umbrella opens: It's drizzling: some people wobble on the damp side-walks. Streetlamps are lit; their reflections shimmer in the puddles. Arm in arm, the night owls walk down a few steps. Here is the black pianist hunched over his keyboard, beads of sweat seeping between the notes. The bass player embraces his instrument, as if it were a jealously loved mistress. The saxophonist has thrown back his head; the notes, C, G, F-sharp, rise and are drawn out, lingering a long time, mingling with the cigarette smoke.

Nox, night, *notte.* Lullabies sung in low voices in children's rooms. Elsewhere in the world, someone is listening to opera. A voice is raised: The Queen of the Night calls for her daughter Pamina.

There is also anxiety, of course, how to forget anxiety, how to silence it? Those awaiting news from missing persons – the unfaithful lover, the soldier fiancé or husband off to war, the issues of which he does not understand, that have nothing to do with him, at the other end of the world, where a minefield is ready to explode beneath his feet. The runaway teenager. People awaiting death, the night of the grave, as they say: eternity. Await it as one awaits deliverance. On death row, in a residence for people losing their independence – some, more cynical, or realistic, call these places homes for the dying, words that chill the soul – or in the hospital, in palliative care, in a bathtub, wrists slashed. Beneath the rubble of destroyed cities. There is anxiety – how to silence it?

Then day dawns – it never falls. A new day in its pink orangey light. With misery? Or with glory.

***

At the End of the World, the terrace is open – at least, a sort of terrace, with three plastic tables that used to be white placed on either side of the entrance of the little St. Zotique Street bistro. Still, for the smokers, it is a marked improvement when summer comes. Three women are there, in fact, Denise and Laure, regulars, and another,

Françoise, who is not. A Diet Coke and two coffees. All three are cheerfully smoking their cigarettes. Tinged with lipstick – coral, raspberry, dark orange, each has her own shade – on the filtered tip. At the second table, Jonathan, a translator who lives in the neighbourhood, nurses a beer. Usually he comes at night, when, after slaving away at his computer for six hours at a stretch, he experiences a sudden a craving for poutine gratinée. But today he is taking advantage of the good weather. Especially given that this year – like every year, in fact – springtime did not measure up to a winter that persisted until May. El Niño was responsible. In the eighteenth century, in Germany, when a frost killed the harvests, the witches were blamed. Thousands of them were burned. There always has to be a scapegoat. Now, sunlight on the nape of his neck, a delicious, almost voluptuous, feeling, Jonathan reads a paperback, sometimes highlighting a word with a fluorescent blue felt-tip pen.

A few posters are glued to the maple tree in front of him. Someone has lost his red-crested cockatoo, a bird who answers to the name of Loulou. Someone else is looking for a grey Angora cat, Dama. A reward is promised in both cases. The third white sheet announces, in capital letters: "HUGE LIQUIDATION. EVERYTHING MUST BE SOLD." An address on Dante Street, not far away, follows. Someone must be about to move.

The third table, for the moment, is unoccupied.

It is four o'clock in the afternoon and the sun shines brightly. It has shone all day. June twenty-one, summer solstice, the longest day of the year.

Inside, well, it's the way it was, or almost. Except that now there are plastic tablecloths with red and white checks, and little vases with rather clever imitation tulips and daisies in the centre. Louison decreed it was time to give the place a modicum of "class." "The neighbourhood is changing; that's why," as she explained to Marjolaine – the dumbfounded chef. "It's called gentrification. It can't be helped."

"Fixation?"

"Fication, Marjolaine. Gentrification. It means that it's not the same type of people living in the neighbourhood. Young people who have gone to university have bought the homes that used to belong to workers. Haven't you noticed?"

She is paid to know it: she sells the houses.

Louison, the boss' new flame. He has separated from the old one – after twenty-seven years of a marriage everyone thought was more or less untroubled – in April, and scarcely three weeks went by before Louison blasted on the scene at the End of the World with her tablecloths and her stacks of CDs. Where did she come from? From a site for lonely hearts? Anything is possible. But three weeks, really … It's indecent, muttered the regulars – card players and taxi drivers – shocked. Do people commit themselves like that after three weeks? The victorious rival, a perfect stranger, is exhibited shamelessly; she is allowed to lay down the law in a place to which the first one – now deserted and repudiated – devoted a good half of her life. Well, not half. But a dozen years, and that counts. And she basically put her stamp on that place. Indecent, revolting – obscene even. According to Marjolaine, there was but one explanation: The adulterous affair had been going on a long time; the legitimate spouse had simply closed her eyes. Denise agreed with her. Men are all the same, she concluded, shrugging her shoulders, disillusioned. And she knew what she was talking about. Women who trust them are ridiculously naive.

That was how Louison turned up at the restaurant, determined to turn everything upside down. A real battle-axe. Playing the radio was out of the question, for example. Because – according to her – those tacky programs drive customers away. That's the whole problem, in fact: If she were trying to drive people away, she would behave no differently. That is, the regular clients, the loyal ones. Louison has plans; that is clear. She aims high.

So she brought her music: Paolina Sanchez and other queens of tango, a bit of reggae, salsa, some old favourites – The Beatles, Joe Dassin – and even the best of Frédéric Chopin, preludes, waltzes and nocturnes. She raised prices: "A $5.95 table d'hôte is for the birds, Charlou. Look around you. With your ridiculous prices, you're headed straight to bankruptcy. We're in a new millennium, in case you hadn't noticed." Charlou! She calls him Charlou in front of the staff – or even Loulou, which takes the cake – and he doesn't bat an eyelid. How can he hope to be respected after that? In any case, the full meal now costs four dollars more and the regular clients find the increase steep despite the flowers and the checkered tablecloths. She had him buy an espresso machine, plus liqueurs and aperitifs that no one drinks. She changed the names of the dishes: the cream of carrot soup is now "velouté crécy," tuna salad is now "chiffonnade gaspésienne" and the regulars can't make head nor tail of it. Moreover, the canned tuna that they buy usually comes from Thailand, a detail that does not seem to bother her.

"Just because things have been working since the dawn of time doesn't mean they shouldn't be changed," she likes to repeat. "Everything can be improved." If you look at it like that, perhaps she is not entirely wrong. "Just because things are calm on the surface doesn't mean they are for the best." No doubt, but when she wanted to call the venerable shepherd's pie "hachis parmentier," Marjolaine rebelled. Enough is enough. "In France, that's what they call it, though," Louison pointed out, refusing to give in. Usually conciliatory, Marjolaine rolled her eyes, teeth and fists clenched. She finds this woman and her decrees hard to swallow. "This isn't France."

"Or else 'cottage pie,'" conceded Louison, vaguely intimidated. "Because shepherd's … well, you have to admit there isn't any lamb in that pie …"

She attempted to joke. "Steak, corn, potato: What's shepherd-like about it?" But Marjolaine hadn't even smiled. She didn't prefer one over the other. The answer was devastating. "Cottage pie or hâchis parmentier or whatever, it's very simple, I'm not making it." As she was on the verge of giving notice, Jean-Charles Dupont – he is the boss, after all – for once stood up for her. There are limits. "A national dish. It's a national dish, Louison. It doesn't change. Same goes for poutine. And too bad if you don't like the name. At the End of the World, we respect tradition." She had been warned, at least for the time being.

Aside from the checkered tablecloths, the tango music, the potted plants – three huge exotic ones that had to be watered once a week, not a drop more – the travel posters on the wall – the Tower of Pisa, the Astronomical Clock in Prague and a sunset in Palma de Mallorca – it is almost the way it had been.

Well, the waitress was a new recruit; that's true. But at the End of the World, it was not unusual to have a new waitress. They never lasted long, so much so that Marjolaine sometimes wonders if young people still want to work. She herself was fifteen when she began working in restaurants and never stopped; she barely takes two weeks holiday a year. Times change, as Louison says. For once, she must be right. As for Marjolaine, she would just as soon that they didn't. Or that they changed more slowly, if change they must.

The one before last, Julie, had simply said: "I've had it," when she left last Tuesday, without even giving a day's notice. Perhaps to return to dance at the Geisha Bar, who knows? Because, before appearing at the End of the World, that's where she'd spent her evenings. There and in other places of ill repute. She was a nude dancer. There is no such thing as a worthless trade and everyone earns their living as best they can. A very sad girl; Marjolaine is not judging her; she had grown attached to her. She knows why Julie was so sad: The man she loved died last winter in a car accident. Hard to learn how to smile again after that.

The new one – she began the day before yesterday – is called Gabriela. Twenty years old, with heavy black eye make-up and crimson lips. A mop of curly black hair fastened on the nape of her neck. A white openwork blouse over a camisole that's also white, a red skirt that shows six inches of tanned thigh, and polka dot ballet shoes. She arrived with her family from El Salvador last winter. She is very good-natured, gets by in French and that's already something. A few customers have said they love her singsong accent. And she didn't flinch when Marjolaine mentioned to her there were dishes to wash. In her family, everyone has to work, so she will do what's needed, especially as it's not particularly demanding. Right now, she is busy filling the salt shakers, the way Marjolaine showed her. Afterwards she'll take care of the pepper shakers, and sugar holders.

The restaurant is almost empty. Except for the four people sitting at tables on the terrace, there is only one client in a corner of the room, scribbling in a lined notebook in front of a lemon tea. As Marjolaine says, ever since he has been coming there – he always drinks two or three cups of tea – he must have filled three hundred notebooks. One day she asked him if he was writing a book and he mumbled something about a comedy or God knows what. If it really is a comedy, people probably won't split their sides laughing when it is staged. The guy doesn't look at all like a humourist. No one has ever seen the ghost of a smile on his narrow face. Except when he discovered the new espresso machine, last May. But Marjolaine didn't handle it well at all; the smile disappeared and hasn't recurred. No, he doesn't smile. The weight of the world on his shoulders, no more no less. And it's heavy. Especially as the poor guy is far from muscular. As thin as a reed and pale as if he'd never seen the sun. Denise nick-named him the Boogeyman, which gives an idea.

But Marjolaine hadn't understood. The man never intended to entertain crowds, quite the opposite. His project – to which he now devotes all his time – is to continue the work of Dante, *The Divine Comedy*, where the poet left off. Like Dante, he began in hell – he's still there. For a while, he too had his Beatrice, a bookseller who read for him about the horrors committed in the last hundred years all over the planet. Betrayals, genocides, rapes and torture, crimes against humanity: the list is endless. Once a week, Beatrice would come in and sum up for him all the defects and barbaric acts of our world. The evening of their last appointment, right here, at the End of the World, the weather was awful; squalls of melting snow, and the poor thing fell on the icy sidewalk. Multiple fractures to her kneecap. She interpreted it as a sign, a warning – that's what she told him when she phoned him from the hospital the next day.

She no longer sees him. She didn't say it outright, but hearing her hesitant voice he understood that she more or less blamed him for her accident. Nevertheless, he continues to ask about her. He knows that, this week, she is resting on an island, Paradise Island. She said that all spring the dampness gave her horrible shooting pain in her wounded knee. The doctor recommended she go to a warm, dry climate. She chose Paradise Island. He objected that the humid weather in the Bahamas was worse than the dampness in Montreal.

She remained silent for a moment. Then: "Paradise to ward off hell," she said finally. She has never seen the sea. Deprived of his muse, he nevertheless advances alone in contemporary hell. When you know that, you understand his melancholy attitude better.

Louison is never there in the afternoon – and the boss also informed her that he wouldn't be in all day – so Marjolaine has turned on the radio. The TV, as usual, is humming on its stand in a corner. Soccer players in green and blue jerseys run after a round ball: a World Cup match somewhere in the world. On the radio, it's time for the news. Floods here, forest fires there. A terrorist attack killed about twenty people in Paris. Another Canadian soldier has died in Afghanistan, the thirteenth victim so far this year. This time, they're claiming it's suicide. Ruddy Wallace, the pedophile killer who called himself Thot, has been executed by lethal injection in the Florida State prison – one less serial killer south of the border. A young Canadian actress has been chosen to play the lead in an American blockbuster. The mundane rubs shoulder with the tragic, as usual.

Nothing very exciting, is happening inside the End of the World. Let's leave Gabriela to her salt shakers, the Boogeyman to his depressing thoughts. Today, outside is where life sparkles. It's the summer solstice, a day of glory. Cars parade down the street, music blasting from their open windows. People stroll unhurriedly on the sidewalk, bare feet in sandals. A few children show off on skateboards, shouting exuberantly, while disabled seniors and others in electric wheelchairs roll along jovially. At one table, three middle-aged women smoke their cigarettes; at another, a translator reads a thriller he will soon begin translating. A translation that, for once, he intends to sign with his real name: Jonathan Jordan. It is time to shed his anonymity. He's fed up with being a ghost translator. From now on, he will take responsibility.

The thriller in question is called *Goddess in Gehenna* and he'll have to find another title in French. *Déesse dans la géhenne* isn't very effective, far from it. What is effective in this case is the plot. Organ trafficking, a pedophile network and a psychopathic killer who makes his victims suffer for a very long time. Some particularly twisted torture is described. Goose bumps guaranteed: Readers are wild for that. In the background, a terrorist group, a multinational pharmaceutical company and a mad chemist who manufactures a virus powerful enough to wipe out the human race. Gehenna, truly. Some information about the place is given in the note at the beginning of the novel: Gehenna used to be the Valley of Hinnom, southwest of Jerusalem; a place where children were sacrificed during unspeakable rituals. Then it was a dumping ground where they constantly burned the city's refuse – as well as the corpses of executed criminals, deemed unworthy of receiving a burial. Lepers and plague victims were relegated there. In the sixteenth century, the word was synonymous with torture. Today, it designates hell. If you believe that such a place exists.

Goddess is the nickname of the officer leading the investigation, a luminous blond who loves caviar and Bloody Marys. Black belt in karate. Doctor of philosophy: Her thesis was on nihilistic thought, Nechayev and company. You wonder what philosophy is doing in this setting – but some folks claim it can lead to anything. Here, the heroine's knowledge helps her predict the acts of the terrorist group. Now the investigators of these new thrillers are less and less likely to be simple police officers. With their array of qualifications, they best each other quoting the most esoteric, most impenetrable thinkers. When they are not computer geniuses. The same applies for the criminals. Disconcerted, readers and translators now must practically be specialists in the same fields to be able to follow all in the twists and turns. The goddess of the novel is called Marina Rosas, Russian on her mother's side, Mexican on her father's. A sort of counterpart to Dante Sullivan, the famous "Jaguar" of the TV series of the same name … Fanny's idol. She swore by him.

All in all, perhaps it wasn't a good idea to have taken on this translation. But he hadn't had a contract since he'd submitted the last one, in January – *Recipes from the Ends of the Earth* by Victor Karr. Just the minutes from committee meetings and other dull platitudes from the Secretary of State. But he should not have taken it on because, now, these excerpts of Nihilist texts – Nechayev and Bakunin are frequently quoted – call to mind a shameful chapter from his past. Which ended up in a suicide attempt. With time, the wounds on his wrists faded, but they are still there. In his memory as well … And he is thinking of Fanny. The pedophiles and psychopathic killers described make him fear the worst.

Fanny, his thirteen-year-old niece, disappeared in Florida last winter. She too saw herself as being committed body and soul to the struggle against crime, later. A profiler, that was all she ever talked about. In Quantico. Or of course in crime scenes in California, with her latex gloves and her blue light, surrounded by athletic investigators. In the forensic team laboratory analyzing everything imaginable, even completely disgusting stuff. What remains of your last meal in your guts, the traces of sperm in your torn anus. She wanted to track down the criminals. It's ironic when you think of it. Ironic and above all poignant.

The inquiry has been stagnating. They haven't found anything, not a clue, not a hair, a drop of blood, an eyelash. A dried tear. Anyway, the case is classified. Jonathan mentally shrugs his shoulders. In Florida, they have other fish to fry, of course. Disappearances: They have dozens of those a day over there. No, reality is totally unlike the detective series on TV. Dante Sullivan and his kind always find something: It's inevitable. But what they find is the killer, once the crime has been committed, Jonathan thinks after a moment. He doesn't want to think about it. He would rather know her dead, he thinks now, dead rather than going through what he is about to translate.

His sister Florence – Fanny's mother – has not recovered. It never rains, it pours: Her husband Robert's adopted daughter said dreadful things about him on a reality TV show. He abused her when she was a child, she fabricated, crocodile tears on her lashes. A web of lies – she ended up admitting it after she was eliminated – but she told them nevertheless.

He turns a page, underlines another world – another computer term. His troubles are not over. While he knows more or less how to use a computer, all those stories of hacking are Greek to him. He looks at his watch. He has an appointment at the End of the World: His friend Mathilde, a translator like himself – now writing her doctoral dissertation in translation studies on Malinche, Cortés' Aztec interpreter – is due to arrive any minute.

The door to the restaurant opens. Marjolaine exits, a cup in one hand, pulls out a chair, and sits down between Denis and Laure. "Coffee and cigarette break," she announces. She takes one from her pack; Laure hands her a pink lighter.

"You sure deserve it," Denise says. "You've worked hard enough."

Marjolaine inhales the smoke luxuriously, head thrown back.

"And what delicious dish have you made for supper?" Denise asks.

"Tuna … I mean *salade gaspésienne*."

The three women burst out laughing. The fourth – Françoise – looks at them uncomprehendingly.

"It's Louison, the boss' new girlfriend, who gives sophisticated names to our grandmothers' recipes," Laure explains. "What did she come up with again for bread pudding?"

"*Pain perdu*, if you please!" Denise says, with a guffaw. "Are we supposed to be impressed? So pretentious."

"And now poor man's pudding should be called warm vanilla cake with maple sauce," Marjolaine says. "She wants me to replace the brown sugar with maple syrup. And it's a dessert invented for poor people. But I see through her machinations. I don't intend to let her boss me around. He knows it."

Françoise emerges from her reverie. "Whom do you mean?"

"Charlou!"

"The boss is called Jean-Charles," Laure explains. "Charlou is his new nickname."

"Even Loulou, sometimes," Marjolaine says. "Unbelievable, I swear."

"Loulou like the lost parrot, you mean?" Françoise asks.

With a movement of her chin, she indicates the cockatoo with pink feathers, crimson crest, perched, looking arrogant, on the poster glued to the tree across from the restaurant. And once again they laugh, Françoise as well.

"Loulou and Louison," Laure says scornfully, in a high-pitched voice.

"Really, some people aren't afraid of looking ridiculous," Denise says.

Gabriela arrives with the coffee pot. "Can I warm you up?" Marjolaine nods, Laure too, but Françoise places her hand over her cup. "Thanks. I've already drunk three, counting my morning coffee. That's enough for today." Gabriela approaches the other table, glances at the beer gone flat. "Care for another beer?" Inspired by his half Mexican goddess, Jonathan orders a Corona with a wedge of lime. And nachos, if they have any. They do not, nor do they have any lime. Then a skinny man with a three-day-old beard, black jeans and T-shirt, settles himself into the third table and orders an iced tea. Marjolaine stares at him. That unkempt beard, that cunning look … she feels as if … she's almost sure, she's already seen him here.

"She doesn't look bad, the new girl," Denise says.

"Good-natured," Marjolaine says. "I don't ask too much of her; I want to give her time to adjust. But I'm hopeful we'll keep her."

"Any news of the other one?"

She is referring to Julie. Marjolaine shakes her head.

"To return to the subject, I tell you the things that Louison comes up with are all for show," Laure says, bursting out. "Her *pain perdu* and her *chiffonnade gaspésienne*."

"Actually, you hadn't finished telling us what's on the menu," Denise says.

"A *velouté Pompadour* …"

The three others exchange stunned looks.

"OK, I'll talk in ordinary language. Cream of cauliflower, spaghetti Bolognese, hamburger steak, mashed …"

"Whipped!" Denise interrupts, beaming.

"Potatoes," Marjolaine says, unruffled.

"Whipped potatoes," Françoise says.

"Accompanying the main dish: sliced tomatoes and cucumbers, radishes and peas. I didn't want to overexert myself today."

"Too nice a day," Françoise says.

"Too nice to stay shut up in a kitchen, especially without air conditioning."

"And for dessert?"

"Three-coloured ice cream or Jell-O, also three colours: red, green, and blue – blueberry flavoured, the first time I've made it. And yesterday's cake – carrot. Half of it's left and carrot cake keeps well. It may even be better the next day. I'm telling you I didn't want to overexert myself ... Oh! I forgot, I also have frozen cod filets. She wanted me to call that ... what was it again? Capillo ... Anyway, that's what they call it in France, apparently."

"Who cares?" Denise says.

A cry from the heart. Jonathan, at the next table, gives a start, disconcerted.

"Who cares what they say in France?"

"I agree with you," Jonathan says, unable to resist. "But I think that your fish is called 'cabillaud' in France."

Mathilde has just arrived. She suppresses her laughter. And Denise keeps going. "It's true, sometimes, for example, you watch a French film and you don't understand a word of what they're saying."

"You're exaggerating," Laure says.

"I am not exaggerating. Has that ever happened to you?"

"Yes," Mathilde says from the other table. "Yesterday evening, in fact. Not a damned word. After half an hour, I turned off the TV."

She bursts out laughing. Jonathan shakes his head. She is talking nonsense.

"You see?" Denise says. "Then after, they have the nerve to put subtitles on our TV shows. That makes me furious. As if we don't speak French as well. Anyway, their ..."

"Cabillaud," Jonathan says again.

"Yes, well, we're not familiar with it; it's not a fish that swims in our waters. And we couldn't care less. Here we eat cod, that's it, that's all, surely Louison is capable of understanding that! She isn't that thick, is she?"

"Not thick," Laure says. "A snob. That's what she is."

Laure crushes her cigarette. Marjolaine lights herself another. "I have time," she says. "All I have to do is put on the potatoes; they're already peeled. Everything's ready." Denise takes out a small mirror from her purse, a tube of coral lipstick and touches herself up.

"I have the feeling she won't be around for long," Marjolaine says. "He'll get fed up."

"Of being called Charlou, you mean?"

"Of being bossed around. Or else she'll get fed up. The way I see it, she has other ambitions. And if I'm not mistaken, she's quite a bit younger than him."

"Not as young as all that," says Laure, categorically. "The wrong side of forty."

"I would have thought younger. Or else she's had work done."

Denise shrugs her shoulders. "You're telling me! Now that she's got her claws into him, plain and simple; do you think she'll let go? She's got him by the balls, plain and simple."

"I have my own views," Marjolaine says. "In my opinion, Madame Dupont still has some cards up her sleeve. She has not had her last word. We've stayed in touch, she and I."

"Anyway, I'd watch my back if I were you," Laure says. "I don't trust that woman at all. I'm talking about Louison, of course. The type who'll smile to your face and stab you in the back."

"I'm not afraid of her."

"If I were you I'd watch out," Laure says.

Françoise glances at her watch. "Six fifteen. I'm going to have to leave."

"What's up? You're in a big hurry!" Denise exclaims. "Is someone waiting for you? A date?"

"That's right. Laugh at me now … Yes, I have a date – with my grandson. Stéphanie asked me to babysit him tonight. Before that, I have to buy groceries; there's nothing in the fridge. Anyway, I'll go pay for my coffee."

Laure taps her on the arm. "Out of the question. Today, I'm treating … But before you leave, there is something I want to talk to you about … Would you like to replace Doris? At our card games, I mean. On Wednesday nights."

"I'll think about it, Laure. I'll think about it. I'm not saying no. Besides, I'm eager to meet Louison."

"Poor Françoise," Marjolaine says, watching her leave then turn onto St. Vallier, heading for the subway.

She heaves a sigh. Two others sigh back.

"Doris' death hit her hard, for sure," Laure says. "Now she's the last one in the family. Of her generation, I mean. She must feel very alone at times."

Doris, Françoise's sister, was felled by an aneurysm in the bathroom at the End of the World six months previously, in the middle of a game of cards, while the snowstorm of the century raged outside.

Marjolaine shakes her head.

"And her daughter lives from hand to mouth," Denise says. "Mother of a young child."

"Not even one year old," Laure says.

"And she's taken up with a good-for-nothing, her too."

Denise must be thinking of the good-for-nothing who made her suffer so much throughout her youth and even longer. A plumber – when he wasn't off living it up – in the company where she had worked as a secretary-accountant. Dead of prostate cancer a few years ago, punished right where he'd sinned – he cheated on her more times than she can count – served him right.

"But maybe she'll take Doris' place at five hundred," Laure says, sounding optimistic. "We can resume our Wednesday card games. Boris and Diderot want to. So does Raoul Potvin."

A taxi pulls up at top speed, parks crooked – the tires squeal and moan – in front of the End of the World. Door slams. Marjolaine shakes her head.

"Speak of the devil," she says.

Diderot Toussaint – a Haitian – exits the car like a lunatic, eyes bulging, brandishing a piece of paper in his left hand. "Day of glory!" he shouts himself hoarse. "Day of glory! Hallelujah! Jesus, Mary and Joseph, thank you!" He stops in front of the three women who are staring at him, dumbfounded, and waves the piece of paper – a lottery ticket – under their noses. "Day of glory!" he repeats, out of breath. "I won!"

A shocked silence follows this declaration. Then:

"The jackpot?" Laure says, stammering.

"Two hundred and three thousand! We have to celebrate! Bring us the best that you have, Marjolaine. Dinner's on me – for everyone."

Drawn by the noise, Gabriela has just appeared at the door of the restaurant.

"Crack open the champagne!" Diderot shouts to her. "Today, nothing is too good!"

"Champagne?"

She looks at Marjolaine, unsure.

"I think Louison left a couple of bottles of sparkling wine in the fridge," Marjolaine says, standing up. "I'll go look."

Denise stands up as well. She thinks sparkling wine would best be drunk inside.

Diderot turns to Mathilde and Jonathan. "Come on, you too," he says. "I'm buying."

The individual with the iced tea has disappeared without warning; no one noticed anything. He left two loonies on the table.

The cork flies off without much fanfare. Diderot pours the sparkling wine into the wine glasses – oddly, Louison did not provide for any flutes or champagne glasses – and brings one to the morose scribbler in his corner. For the first time, a smile lights up the stern face.

"If I understand correctly, you just won the lottery? My congratulations, sir."

"Diderot. Diderot Toussaint."

"A beautiful name."

Glasses clink; everyone speaks at once.

"What do you intend to do with the cash?" Laure asks.

"For starters, I'll buy my taxi. From now on, I'm my own boss. And part of it will go to Haiti. That's the least I can do."

Murmurs of approval greet this generous promise. Haiti always needs help, and now more than ever.

Marjolaine announces that she can make a huge shepherd's pie. "I have everything I need. Gabriela will give me a hand." Otherwise, they have the choice between spaghetti or pan-fried cod with vegetables. They opt unanimously for the shepherd's pie. Both disappear into the kitchen. "I'm going to call the Savine brothers on their cell phones," Diderot says. "They really must come too."

Fédor and Boris Savine, taxi drivers, who have haunted the End of the World since the dawn of time. Boris is one of their card-playing partners. Raoul Potvin as well, but strangely, Diderot has not mentioned him.

"I spoke to Boris," he says. "He's coming later. Fédor didn't answer."

19

Then Gabriela sets out bowls of chips and pickles on the counter, crackers and cubes of orange-coloured cheese stabbed with multi-coloured toothpicks.

On the radio, the program *Bonsoir, nostalgie* – that for two hours plays special requests from listeners – has just begun. Against all expectations, an operatic aria is broadcast. This is definitely a first. *Der Hölle Rache kocht in meinem Herzen.*

"*The Magic Flute,*" Jonathan says. "The Queen of the Night aria."

Denise shrugs her shoulders.

"Hell's vengeance boils in my heart …" the melancholy writer translates. "Sung by Edita Grurberová, I think. To my mind, the best queen of all time … Perhaps even under the direction of Nikolaus Harnoncourt."

Jonathan leans over toward Mathilde, murmurs that it is perhaps a request from his sister Florence.

"You sister calls to request songs, music I mean, from opera, on the radio?"

She seems stunned.

"That's all she listens to; the children can't stand it anymore." He sighs. "Neither can I."

"If she listens to it all the time, why request it on the radio?"

"She has strange ideas … It would be easier to tell you what she doesn't do … but I may be wrong."

Laure listens with solemn intensity.

"Anyway, personally, I can't say I don't find that beautiful," she declares after a moment.

"Is there any more bubbly?" Diderot asks in the direction of the kitchen. "Tonight I can drink as much as I want; I've stopped for the night. Anyway, I'm too excited; I'd be liable to have an accident."

Seven thirty. The program is suddenly interrupted by a special news bulletin: Among the victims of the suicide bombing in Paris, there is one Canadian, seven Americans. Then Paul Anka and his Diana follow the Queen of the Night. A strange combination. The least that can be said is that nostalgia is eclectic this evening.

The second cork flies off with no more fanfare. Sparkling wine fills the glasses. Hands reach for the crackers, tongues loosen, conversations become animated. Gabriela brings a bowl of radishes cut into flowers.

On the TV, a couple – she, a redhead, hair in a bob, eyes too green (coloured lenses, no doubt), he, a tanned beefcake in a suit and tie – also drink champagne in a living room straight out of a trendy décor magazine advertisement.

Denise approaches the taciturn writer – but is he a writer? "Hi, I'm Denise," she says. "And you, what's your name?"

He hesitates a moment, then: "The Boogeyman," he replies.

Denise remains speechless, which is rare for her. He reassures her. "Don't worry. I'd even say I find it funny."

"That's good, because we just said it for a laugh," she stammers, mortified. Then, unable to repress her curiosity: "What do you write all day long in your notebooks?"

"It's not important."

She insists: "A book?"

"If you like. But I'd be amazed if you read it one day."

"Why do you say that? Do I look like someone who doesn't know how to read?"

"Because it won't be published in my lifetime."

They had been right to find him strange, Denise tells herself: This man spends his days writing to be read after his death.

On the radio, an old familiar song, *Broken Wings* – the theme song from the cult film, requested at least once a month. This evening, a jazzy version. "It's like *La vie en rose*," Jonathan says to Mathilde. "People don't tire of it."

"Or *Ne me quitte pas*."

Marjolaine emerges from the kitchen.

"The shepherd's pie is in the oven," she announces. "Sit down We're bringing the soup … excuse me, the *velouté Pompadour*." Then she stands still. "I've got it!"

"What have you got?" Denise asks.

"That guy, there, the one who was drinking iced tea on the terrace. He was here the evening when … the evening when Doris …"

"The evening she died?"

"He was there. That time too, he was drinking tea. Not iced, obviously. It was twenty below zero. Don't you remember?"

Denise thinks. Now that she thinks of it, it really could be him, she says. Sitting at that table over there near the window. "He was drinking tea," Marjolaine says again. "I recognized him. I would swear on it." Laure doesn't remember. Nor does Diderot.

Gabriela sets down paper placemats and the cutlery. "Set a place for Marjolaine and yourself as well," Diderot says. "Everyone is invited." The pale writer excuses himself; he can't stay. He has work to finish. He leaves at the moment that Raoul Potvin makes his entrance.

Raoul scans the room, gives a long whistle when he notices the wine glasses, the radish flowers and the crackers.

"Is it somebody's birthday?"

Denise quickly fills him in.

"Diderot is celebrating," she says. "He won the jackpot."

"What do you mean, the jackpot?"

"The lottery," Laure says. "He won two hundred and three thousand. Is that right, Diderot?"

"Not the jackpot," Diderot says. "The jackpot is about ten million."

"He's going to buy his taxi."

Raoul remains silent for a moment, frowning, as if not sure he understood. Usually Diderot and he buy lottery tickets together.

"If you won, that means I won as well," he says – and his face lights up. "Half. One hundred and one thousand … One hundred and one thousand five hundred."

"Actually, no, Raoul." Diderot clears his throat. "Our numbers didn't come up."

All of a sudden, he looks uncomfortable. No one speaks.

"I bought a second ticket," he explains, finally. Then, turning to Gabriela: "Bring a glass of wine for my friend Raoul."

"I don't want any wine!"

He sits down heavily. "Bring me a beer," he says. "And I'm still able to pay for my own."

Gabriela complies, uneasy. Embarrassed, Mathilde motions to Jonathan that they had better slip out. She feels as if they're becoming embroiled in a dilemma that does not concern them, a scene that could end in disaster. But Jonathan is intrigued.

"And you were going to celebrate without even telling me."

Raoul now feels as if he's the victim of a plot: Everyone is betraying him.

"I was going to phone you," Diderot says.

"It seems to me … it's fine to say we're friends, but that's not enough. We have an agreement," he says, looking Diderot straight in the eye. "When two people buy a lottery ticket together, the winnings should be shared."

"I told you, our ticket didn't win. I bought another one."

"There was never talk of our buying tickets separately, on our own."

"Come on, Raoul," Laure says. "I think you're being unfair. Nothing prevented Diderot from buying a ticket. You could have, too. We live in a free country."

"I didn't ask you!"

Gabriela looks at Marjolaine: "Shall I bring the soup now?"

Marjolaine seizes the opportunity to create a diversion. She is afraid the celebration will turn sour. You never know what to expect when Raoul Potvin is there.

"My God! The Pompadour!" she exclaims. "We can't let our marquise get cold. That would be very bad form."

But Raoul is no mood for joking. He begins his refrain anew: They are partners; they must share equally. That's the law; he is sticking to his guns.

"You always were a sore loser," Laure says.

"I'm not a sore loser! The only thing I will not put up with is cheating."

"Don't talk like that," Denise says. "Diderot did nothing dishonest."

"Well, I call that cheating. There's no other word."

"Listen, if you don't believe me, see for yourself," Diderot says. "The numbers are my mother's birthday."

He takes the winning ticket out of his pocket, hands it to Raoul.

"Don't give it to him!" Denise shouts.

But it's too late. Raoul has lit his lighter. And before six pairs of incredulous eyes, two hundred and three thousand dollars are immediately – in less than five seconds – reduced to smoke and ash.

2

By the Riverside,
Stabbed in the Back

Louison, the boss' new flame.
The type who'll smile to your face
and stab you in the back.

"To begin with, we'll have to find a chef," she says.

There she goes again. The discussion has been going on for two long months. For him, the subject is closed. But not for her.

"We already have Marjolaine," he says, for the umpteenth time. "She does a good job, to my mind."

"Marjolaine!"

She rolls her eyes to the sky. The corners of her lips turn down; it looks as if she's going to spit. Contempt incarnate. He may well be crazy about her, but when she makes that face – which is far too often, to his mind – he is not so sure of his feelings.

"Your former waitress!" she says, spitting out the words. "I wonder what she's doing at the stove. I'm talking about a chef worthy of that name."

He shrugs his shoulders. "What she's doing is cooking," he replies, exasperated. "And the customers are satisfied."

"Well, they're not hard to please, then."

He finds her particularly vicious today. She's gotten up on the wrong side of the bed again. Or something's eating her; perhaps she was stung by a hornet first thing. Yet she was all sweetness and light when she awoke. Her mood has changed and he doesn't know why. Perhaps she's bipolar? Or going through menopause, like his sister-in-law, Diane. He can't think of anything else. What he sees is that she isn't easy to follow. With her, you never know where you stand. Shilly-shallying. He trembles when he tries to predict the next step.

"You have something against her because of that shepherd's pie business, admit it," he says, trying to joke.

"Shepherd's pie! Do people go out to eat when they want shepherd's pie? I don't, that's for sure."

She rolls her eyes again – a habit with her – and begins her old refrain. She says no, when you go out, it's for a change of scenery. You look for something new, variety, a bit of excitement! To spice up your humdrum day-to-day life, that's what you look for. You want an elegant decor, food you wouldn't be able to make yourself. Refined, exotic, ethnic. You want to be surprised. Seduced. In short, you want a dream. Because, he must admit, along with her, that without dreaming our existence really would be miserable. Reality is often challenging. To end up with the same ambiance, the same shepherd's pies and other poor men's pudding from childhood – too often underprivileged – why not stay at home listening to boring radio, TV, and if you don't feel like cooking, have a pizza delivered, it's as simple as that. And less expensive.

"What I'm saying is that your Marjolaine has no creativity," she says in a tone that brooks no reply.

"I'm not asking her for much," he says, wearily. "And the clients seem to like it."

"Let's talk about your clientele! Two or three old ladies, some foul-mouthed taxi drivers."

Difficult to claim otherwise. But he doesn't intend to give in without putting up a token fight.

"Even old ladies and taxi drivers are entitled to enjoy themselves. And to eat what they want. I provide a kind of home for them, a place where they feel comfortable."

"Very charitable of you, I'm sure. But you should know that business and charity have never been a good match."

"You wouldn't be a bit of a snob, Louison?"

"It's true, I'm a snob," she says. "But can you tell me what they eat, your old ladies?"

"What they eat? Well, they …"

She cuts him off. "You don't make a penny profit off them. They cost you more than they bring in. They spend hours chatting in front of a Diet Coke or a coffee. Regular."

This last word is uttered with rage: The espresso machine of which she is so proud – a Gaggia made in Italy – is basically never used. Marjolaine barely knows how it works. And as for the *crema*, it's not even worth discussing it.

In fact, he has yet come to terms with the exorbitant price of the machine that isn't used. Whereas the good old filter coffee maker satisfied and still satisfies the regulars: They can have two – or even three – refills, though some overdo it, not spending another cent. Nevertheless, he tries to play for time.

"Anyway, there aren't just old ladies, as you say. To listen to you, you'd think I was running a golden age club. I have quite a few young people, for example, who come after the bars close for poutine or even for breakfast: eggs, bacon, toast, coffee."

"Another thing we'll have to change. In my opinion, there's no profit in remaining open all night to serve a few poutines and other inexpensive stuff."

"It's not only young people. You'd be surprised at the number of people who are hungry at night … Police officers, bartenders, ambulance drivers, journalists. To name but a few. Not to mention the insomniacs. For example, I have a translator who comes regularly at around three o'clock in the morning."

"Journalists at the End of the World? That surprises me."

For him, in the end, making a profit doesn't matter. As long as he meets his costs. With a little left over.

"We've always been open at night," he says. "It's our …" – he searches for the word – "vocation. For ages, you must know that the End of the World has been a Montreal institution."

"Perhaps," she says, "but most of the time, the young people you describe arrive drunk, make noise. When they're not drug dealers: crack, coke, and what have you."

"Never noticed."

Which is not quite true. It's just that he prefers not to see certain things. She shrugs her shoulders.

"Obviously, you go through life with your eyes closed. But all that damages our reputation, you know as well as I. Neighbours have complained, and on more than one occasion."

As usual when they broach this delicate topic, they go round in circles, each unwilling to compromise.

"Didn't we decide to take the day off?" he asks. "We really could forget about work for a day, you know."

True, this morning, she had decreed: "Today I have no appointments. Let's celebrate the solstice. I won't even bring my cell phone." Beautiful weather had been forecast all day. And after the dreadful spring they'd had – rarely more than eleven miserable degrees in May, if that, and in June it had rained almost every day, not to mention the rivers bursting their banks across the country – he didn't feel like working either. She sent him out to buy champagne while she prepared a picnic: raw milk cheeses, prosciutto, wild strawberries and walnut bread. "Real champagne, Charlou, not sparkling wine," she had said. "And two bottles. No, three."

Charlou, that is Jean-Charles Dupont, owner of the End of the World. And he didn't find Louison on a site for lonely hearts. Justine, his wife – now his ex-wife – had been pestering him for months to sell the cottage where even their children didn't have time to go anymore. He finally gave in and called on the services of Constance Julien. More precisely, Constance-Louise. Her parents couldn't agree on the first name – her mother wanted Louise, her father was dead set on Constance, a young sister who died very young – they made the compromise when she was born. On her professional cards, on the signs on properties to sell – yes, she's a real estate agent – it's Constance Julien. Because three first names in a row is a bit much. And as she likes to remind her clients: "Constancy inspires confidence." Her trademark: constancy. As for the rest, it's Louison, more simply. Two identities: one for work, the other for feelings. But the former, that of the ambitious businesswoman, is always on the lookout, the former never sleeps.

That's how their love began. You wake up one morning not thinking that everything in your life is going to change. The hurricane you didn't predict is suddenly unleashed. And when it's unleashed, it destroys your past, without mercy. Everything will soon fall to pieces, fall apart, everything will fly away. Wife, children, cottage, house. This existence – habits, complacency, peculiar quirks, inoffensive or not – that we thought more or less unclouded. Real chaos. You don't know, though, not yet. You go about your business as usual.

Did it really happen that way? A storm lay waste to everything? Almost, let's say. The thing was not so far-reaching, of course. But we're not in a novel. Here, none of the agony accompanied by high fever, epileptic seizures and fainting with which Tolstoy, Dostoevsky and their followers burdened their characters. Neither Jean-Charles nor Louison have Slavic souls. Fortunately. Their storm was more akin to a spring shower, melting snow accompanied by gusts of wind more unpleasant than violent.

Justine of course protested and cried – she is still crying; the children, Vanessa and Pierrick, sided with their mother. Luckily, Kim wasn't there when the events occurred. She had taken a gap year after Cegep and was roaming around Europe with her backpack. In Italy, according to the latest news. Marjolaine had also taken sides, though less ostentatiously in her case. As for the customers – the regulars – their silences and sighs speak volumes. Things will calm down eventually, Jean-Charles Dupont knows. After the rain, the sun comes out and all that. Stereotypes, no doubt, but they have proved to be true. Popular wisdom is and will always be the most reliable. Yes, everything will fall into place. You just have to give it time.

It was morning. They were discussing the terms of the contract when suddenly it struck him. Constance Julien was his type of woman, exactly his type – Justine no longer was and hadn't been for several years. But Constance … svelte, elegant – a salmon-coloured cashmere sweater that morning, a flowing print skirt that, how to say, moved when she moved – mid-length hair, a pretty chestnut brown with mahogany highlights. So this was what they call love at first sight. Enthralled – there is no other word to describe his condition.

And it happened to him right in the middle of the morning – usually, people associate this kind of commotion with night-time – in a realtor's office, while she was filling in a form, asking down-to-earth questions that he tried to answer as best as possible.

First of all, he found her beautiful. Physical attraction plays a key role in love at first sight, but in this case, it was more than that. It felt transcendent and went beyond Constance Julien's appearance. There was the scent, a smell both floral and musky that had made his head spin. There was the voice. The importance of the voice in stories of seduction is never emphasized enough. Constance's was deeper than high, a bit husky that day – she was recovering from laryngitis. A real caress. And the confident, relaxed attitude: She was in full possession of her faculties, without that aggressive side that salespeople too often have. Even her habit of constantly caressing her left wrist with her right thumb he found irresistible. She was – she is – all that Justine is not, it must be said.

He invited her to lunch. An impulse. To tell the truth, selling the cottage had been the least of his worries; his mind was no longer on numbers. And she who – at least, that's what she claimed – never accepted invitations from her clients – mustn't mix business and feelings – accepted. The same impulse.

He hadn't invited her to the End of the World, far from it. Strangely, in Constance's presence, with her skirt that seemed alive, her sweater like a second skin – even her umbrella looked like it had a designer label – it was as if he were ashamed, all of a sudden, of his unpretentious bistro. No, he took her instead to a fashionable – and expensive – French restaurant downtown where he was unlikely to meet anyone he knew. Well beyond his means. But his mind was no longer on numbers, as we've said.

He almost ordered escargots, which he adores, but the idea of garlic butter – and his breath after eating them – made him quickly change his mind. More wisely, he ordered a soup – carrot – she, a salad called chiffonnade, mesclun, slices of pear, shaved parmesan, roasted hazelnuts. In the middle of the main dish – hanger steak with four kinds of pepper for him, for her (she eats light at lunch) an omelette with chanterelles – she suggested they call each other by their first names.

They finished the bottle of Chablis. With the coffee – despite the enticing names, they deemed dessert superfluous – they ordered digestives, a fine Napoleon for him – that day, nothing was too good, he was in the mood to celebrate – Chartreuse for her. When the last sip was drunk, she said: "You can call me Louison if you like."

Simple – and ordinary – adultery had not been contemplated for a single moment. Louison put her cards on the table from the start: all or nothing. He hadn't hesitated. Or not for long.

Everything happened quickly and it was barely one month later that Jean-Charles separated from Justine – after twenty-seven years – and moved into Louison's condo on the Plateau, a place she shared before with an old, rather ill-tempered Siamese cat named Lolita. The thing was not yet official, but if they reach an agreement, and they will, he will leave the house and everything in it to Justine and keep the End of the World for himself. They will split the profits from the sale of the cottage. When it sells, which has not yet happened.

And since it has not, he would rather avoid bringing Louison there.

Today, they are in a house in the Laurentians on the river, in Sainte-Marguerite. Louison fumbles in the kitchen drawers. "Where could they have put the placemats?"

"Are you sure we're entitled to be here?"

He looks around him, concerned. He feels a bit uncomfortable in this strange house. As if someone, the owner, or even, in the worst case, the police could suddenly burst in and surprise them.

Now it's she who shrugs her shoulders. "I have his keys, Charlou. He gave me carte blanche. He trusts me completely."

"One of your many suitors?"

"A client. And you know I'm not the type to mix business with feelings. You were the exception to the rule. I wonder if I was well inspired that day … Don't make that face. I'm joking, Loulou."

She adds that the client in question is a former university professor – which explains the number of books here. "I sold his house in Montreal a couple of years ago. Now he claims he's bored in the country. Not enough distractions. People are never happy. I'm not complaining. With the dissatisfied, I earn my living ... For the moment, he's somewhere in Europe, I'm not sure where exactly. He talked about Prague, Vienna and Paris. He won't be back before September."

"Some people are lucky."

"Everyone can be lucky ... It's okay, I found them. The placemats. Could you open the champagne? The glasses are on the sideboard."

He opens the bottle and fills two flutes without spilling too much of it.

"You have to know how to attract luck," Louison says, raising her glass. "To our good health, Loulou! You have to seize opportunities, that's all. *Carpe diem*, as the saying goes ... Speaking of which ... Wouldn't you like to go on a trip, next summer, for instance? Two weeks, just you and me, in Paris? No, in Italy, in Tuscany." She stares into space for a moment – who knows what experiences she had over there, and with whom. "I would so like to see Tuscany again."

Jean-Charles has never seen it. He has not had a lot of time – or the urge, to tell the truth – to travel. The restaurant, the house, the cottage, two weeks down south in winter, in Florida usually, but also in Cuba, in the Dominican Republic – in Cabarete, just once, neither he nor Justine liked it – just about sums up his knowledge of the vast world. Not a stellar track record, all in all. Perhaps the time has come to expand his horizons.

"I'm not saying no. If we sell the cottage."

"We'll sell it."

***

Later – they'd eaten, drunk a bottle of champagne, opened the second – Louison starts in again. The End of the World is in a strategic place, she said, just next to Little Italy, in a rapidly gentrifying neighbourhood. "Do you even realize what you have in your hands?"

He never really thought about it. All the same, he nods his head.

"A gem, and you're not taking advantage of it."

It can no longer really be described as a working-class neighbourhood, she continues. All you have to do is walk around the lanes and glance at the landscaped yards: Flower beds of annuals have re-placed the tomato plants of times past. Everyone on their treated wood deck. There are countless cheese shops, chocolate shops and small bakeries. Shops with trendy knick-knacks are sprouting up like mushrooms; fashion designers are now well established on a nearby street. The Jean-Talon market has become a must, the place where everyone wants to be seen buying their organic fruit and vegetables, their sustainable fish and their wild mushrooms. That's why the time has come to seize the opportunity and revamp the End of the World. Others have done it. He has already waited too long.

"You never let up."

"If I let up, I wouldn't have succeeded in my profession."

She says that checked tablecloths and plastic flowers were only a beginning. To get people used to the fact that the decor will change. It's always better to do things gradually. She recommends the gentle method. Abrupt changes make people panic; it's a fact. They'll begin by repainting. This summer, over the vacation, they'll close for a few weeks. Those beige walls are depressing. They need colour – she's thinking of vibrant orange, to get off the beaten path – a huge mirror behind the counter for the illusion of depth. She knows workmen who will make him a good price. As for the tourist posters, she doesn't want to stop there either. They could think of something more … I don't know … more attention-getting, exhibitions of paintings, for example. There are is no shortage of artists and most are longing to find places to exhibit. At the vernissages, they would serve rosé wine and verrines, which are very trendy. They could offer jazz evenings, a slunch late on Sunday afternoons, no one does that. "You know, little sweet and savoury treats that they serve with smoothies, cocktails or tea. It's very … playful."

"Playful?"

"Well, yes, it's playful. People want to have fun, I told you. Be-sides, no one brunches anymore. The concept is outdated."

All these plans make him a bit dizzy. She calls him a dreamer, yet it is she who spends her time dreaming. She keeps building all these castles in the air. As if life, the way it is, cannot satisfy her.

He suggests going out. The afternoon is still young.

"A walk through the trees along the river, what do you say?"

The birdsong, he thinks, the flawless blue sky – he feels in a poetic mood – the trees of the quaking aspen that tremble in the breeze, so moving, that trembling. There is a blanket in the trunk of the car. They could ... No, she says. Too dangerous. There are bears in the area and one could attack them. Apparently there's a shortage of berries this year. The frustration makes them aggressive. Not to mention wasps, to which she is allergic. She doesn't intend to end the day in the emergency room. She has other plans. She brought a cookbook, the latest Victor Karr – it's just come out. It could give her an idea of the menus they could offer. "Look, Exotic Turkey, for example, also known as Turkey from the End of the World. A name tailor-made for us ... In fact, congratulations. You had an inspired idea when you gave your restaurant that name."

"Can't take any credit. It was already called that when I bought it."

Twelve years earlier. Before that, he was a truck driver. But Justine found the weeks long when he went to deliver all sorts of things to the other end of Canada, sometimes even to the United States.

"It's still a great find for a little neighbourhood restaurant. The name will help us ... So back to the turkey. Look at the photo. Appetizing, don't you think? It's made with mangoes, plantains and almonds. Flambé with Cointreau. Served with saffron rice decorated with edible flowers: nasturtiums and poppies. Can you imagine Christmas Eve?"

"Nasturtiums," he says, sighing. "In December."

"Eggnog to start the evening," she says, not letting herself get flustered, "It's English; eggnog with brandy in it. We end with a typically French dessert, Bûche de Noël, a chestnut log topped with a coulis of Saskatoon berries, for the Canadian side ..." Then she says as he looks abashed: "The berries are like cranberries."

There would be candles in every colour on the tables and tango music would provide a romantic atmosphere to the evening. "We could try to find a bandoneon player. As for *Petit papa Noël* and *O Holy Night*, I don't know about you, but I for one can't stand them anymore ... It would be a change from the never-ending tourtières,

34

mashed potatoes and peas. And with that kind of menu, the restaurant would be jammed. We'd be turning away people, believe me."

He shakes his head, not convinced.

"Again, these are only ideas," she says. "No question of copying recipes. The chef will invent some."

"I don't know, Louison. At the End of the World, the traditional Christmas Eve meal has always been successful."

When he uses this type of logic, he exasperates her. She wants to shake him. Time goes by, things evolve while he … sometimes it's as if he sees nothing. He is clinging to a past that no longer exists. She tells him as much. "You are completely out of date, Charlou."

"Maybe. I was just hoping that you liked me the way I am."

Now he's bringing love into the picture. Being emotional. Impossible to have a discussion with him.

"Love has nothing to do with it," she says. "You know full well that I love you, Loulou. The way you are. That doesn't stop me from seeing your weaknesses. If I didn't love you, why do you think I would be here today with you when I could earn twenty thousand dollars selling a house? Why would I agree for you to come live with me? But here we are talking about traditions. I tell you that they are there to be shaken up. The magic word from now on is fusion."

He announces that he's going out for a little walk; he's not afraid of bears. Besides, he doesn't intend to venture very far. Just get some air, smoke a cigarette or two.

As he is walking and smoking, he thinks. There is some truth in what Louison says. Perhaps he could have been more watchful. He did not see – or want to see – the changes that were occurring; he does not deny it. It's just that she's going too fast. Expeditious. Though in bed, it's the opposite; she can take an hour to reach orgasm. At least, he thinks it's an orgasm. Perhaps she has just had enough.

"Not a shadow of a bear on the horizon," he says when he returns.

"You didn't go far enough. So much the better … And I took advantage of your absence to think."

"My, my."

35

"I have a client who teaches at the Institut d'hôtellerie," she continues, insensitive to the sarcasm. "I'll ask him to suggest the best candidate."

"I can't afford it, Louison," he says. "I can't afford a chef from the Institut, especially one at the top of his class. I can barely manage to pay Marjolaine. Minimum wage. And with what the divorce is going to cost me …"

She doesn't seem to realize. Just the three bottles of – real – champagne earlier … whereas he prefers red wine and there are excellent ones at half the price. She is not being sensible. Her grandiose ideas sometimes scare him. If it continues, he'll end up missing the quiet life he had with Justine.

"I'm not as rich as you," he says – and it mortifies him.

If it's chauvinistic to be mortified by that, so be it. You can't change your personality. Though with Louison, he doesn't often have an opportunity to be chauvinistic. She's the dominant one in their relationship. And that too hurts his pride.

"Who says you'll pay for everything, Loulou? I wanted to surprise you, but I might as well tell you know: I'm thinking of investing in your business. I've almost had enough of selling houses. With the crisis prices may rise, but solvent buyers are harder and harder to find. And the ones you find need a lot of persuading to pay the asking price … When the restaurant becomes profitable – I give us a year – I plan to slow down. Maybe even stop."

Change vocations. Constance Julien, owner of the End of the World, the restaurant where the food is so wonderful, she dreams. She's imagining new things, molecular cuisine, for example. But better to wait, she knows. Charlou – not to mention his customers – is certainly not ready to accept such upheaval. To begin with, give things a big boost: new decor, new menu, a chef who is adventurous. Word of mouth will do the rest. Yes, a year, no more.

***

Later, in the bed of John Paradis – the name of the retired professor.

They drank too much to drive; they'll spend the night here. Perhaps even drank too much, at least in Jean-Charles' case, to make love.

36

He's felt drained since earlier, scarcely managing to stifle his yawning. His eyelids weigh a ton. Actually, he imagined another way of celebrating the solstice. He's disappointed.

Louison takes the remote control from the night table and turns on the TV. The news is on. Another terrorist attack, for which no one has yet claimed responsibility, has claimed more than twenty lives in an upscale bar in Paris. Distressing images follow one another on screen: the wounded on stretchers, terrified faces and a lone bloodied shoe amid the rubble.

"You see," Louison shouts, triumphantly. "That's what I told you: *carpe diem*. Life is short, too short. You never know what's waiting for you around the corner ... and you're not even fifty."

"Almost. I'll be fifty on September 21. But I really don't see the connection between my age and the terrorist attacks."

"The connection is that we only have one life, Charlou, we have to live it when it is here. How do you want to spend yours? As an owner of a greasy spoon until the end of your days? ... What you lack is ambition."

He agrees. Justine herself criticized him for it sometimes. But she put on white gloves to do so.

"We'll put it right," Louison says. "Trust me. We have three months to set everything in place. We'll jazz it up, our End of the World ... The most important thing is to find a chef."

"How do you think I'm going to explain that to Marjolaine?" he says. "Turfing her out after all those years of loyal service."

"You don't have to justify yourself. You're the boss, Charlou; you can do what you want. Do you think they have feelings like that in big companies? When they want to rationalize, when they want to optimize, well then they rationalize and optimize, that's it."

She places her hand on the side of his neck, slides a finger behind his ear. "And you'll admit that in the beginning I was full of good will toward her." She begins to scratch gently with her blood-red nail. "But little by little she ruins everything I try to improve. She's dead set against me."

On this point, it's impossible to contradict her. Marjolaine makes no effort and the atmosphere in the restaurant is anything but harmonious when Louison is there. Very often nowadays, especially in the evenings.

"Of course, she's taken Justine's side. Well, I understand her. It's a question of loyalty in her case. They were quite close. I wouldn't be surprised if they've kept in touch."

He says it without too much conviction. For if Marjolaine's loyalty, if it can be called that, explains her attitude, it still does not justify it. She is loyal to Justine, but she is working for him. And for Louison, who is now nibbling the lobe of his other ear. Hard to resist.

"It still breaks my heart to do that to her."

He is speaking in the present, as if it were already done.

"Now you're being dramatic, Loulou ... She isn't as pitiful as all that. She'll be entitled to unemployment for at least a year. And we can give her severance pay if it will help you feel less guilty." Then she softens: "I know what you're feeling. In a way, I even sympathize with Marjolaine."

"You?"

"My heart is not made of iron. Of stone I mean."

"It's as if you're asking me to stab her in the back," he mumbles.

But soon he will surrender; he's already waving the white flag. Marjolaine doesn't have a chance. Especially as Louison's hand is now running down his chest, toward his belly button, and farther. All of a sudden, he's not tired anymore.

3

Beginning of a Sleepless Night
in Marina di Pisa

*People who are awaiting death, the
night of the grave, as they say,
eternity.
"I would so like to see Tuscany
again."*

He wanted to see Tuscany again. Ernesto Liri – almost one hundred years old, inactive musician since he was half his age – had been whining for months. "My Tuscany. Do you understand, it's my childhood, my origin … my Santiago de Compostela pilgrimage … My final dream. It's my final hope." Anything at all, in fact, in every tone of voice imaginable – usually whining, tearful, even vengeful. They tried to reason with him: He had not been in at least thirty years; everything would have changed over there. He wouldn't recognize anything anymore, he would be disappointed, disoriented at best. Why take such a risk? So often memory embellishes; we idealize the past, it's been proven. Let him keep his memories intact. He nodded his head without much conviction. The following day, he would begin anew. "Tuscany is where I was born. I came into the world there, you see. I have so many memories."

"They are your treasure."

"When you're on the point of knocking on heaven's door the way I am, treasure is an illusion."

"You could live another ten years. At least."

But living another ten years was not something he wanted. Not in his condition. He really was in a pitiful state – white with age, trembling, half deaf, and completely deaf when he didn't wear his hearing aid, practically impotent, lost most of the time. If he hadn't been as rich as he was, he would have been relegated to an old people's home with others like him who were losing their independence.

"I want to see the olive trees again," he said. "I want to see the Arno again. One last time."

"The Black Sea is right in front of you. What more could you ask for?"

"The Mediterranean."

"The Black Sea is surely just as inspiring. Few people are lucky enough to be able to look out on it every day. You're one of the fortunate. Don't complain."

He shook his head. "I want to walk in the steps of Dante." Walk? The poor man was confined to a wheelchair. "The final dream of a dying old man. You can't refuse me. You wouldn't be that cruel. Otherwise, I'll be leaving this world with a tormented soul." How to respond to that? He was being melodramatic. He even went so far as to compare himself to a salmon returning to spawn in the river where its mother had laid her eggs. Bulgaria, with its roses and the sight of this Black Sea that he used to love so much, was no longer enough.

They ended up giving in. Stefan to begin with – he too had a great desire to travel to Italy – then Doctor Markov, having run out of arguments, and finally the family, having run out of patience. "Well, let him go since he wants to so badly. But above all, his whining must stop. We can't take it anymore." They had gotten on the road at dawn on his ninety-seventh birthday. The car trip from Nessebar to Sofia, then one flight – first class – to Pisa. A very full day for such a frail man. But he had held up, carried along by his dream.

Stefan, secretary, companion, chauffeur, confidant – and clandestine biographer in fits and starts, when his duties left him the time – and Yuri, masseur and nurse, both indispensible companions, were of course on the odyssey.

He wanted to see Tuscany again, and now it seemed as if he would never leave it. Exiting the room earlier, the doctor murmured that he would not survive the night. He said it in Italian, *non passerà la notte*, but Stefan understood. He manages quite well now. He has been taking intensive Italian classes since they settled in Marina di Pisa. But he would have understood without even speaking the language. Ernesto Liri's death rattles do not lie. The old man is on the point of death.

Stefan is seated at the dying man's bedside. A light, scented breeze – night flowers – enters through the open window. A television sits on a table in one corner: the DVD of *Broken Wings* has been playing constantly since early evening. The idea was Laura's, Liri's youngest daughter. She thinks that playing the film that made him famous will ease his passage into the next world. Hearing his iconic music will soothe him, she says. But Stefan wonders. He also wonders if the dying man can hear it. He glances at the screen. It is now the scene – a cult scene in a cult film – where Lola runs along an alleyway at night, on the verge of breaking the heel of her shoe. She wants to warn Stephen, her beloved, that Bromsky, the éminence grise of the story – more black than gray, in fact – has decided to kill him.

There are two cult scenes: the one with the broken heel – some filmmakers have recreated it with variants, a tip of the hat to the venerated master – and the last, the one most often cited. Lola, in a straight skirt and white blouse – no torrid embracing in the film, scarcely two or three chaste kisses, no nudity, and Lola is always dressed, modestly even – is standing in front of her mirror, a tube of red lipstick in her hand. She will write *Forgive me*. And for over half a century, the same question remains: Who is Lola asking to forgive her? Generally, people think it is Stephen, whom she betrayed without wanting to. But nothing is clear.

Even Liri had no answer. He once implied that it was Marjorie Martinez herself – the actress portraying Lola – who insisted on writing these words on the mirror: She was asking forgiveness from the child she did not bring into the world. Their child.

His eyelids tremble. What is he thinking about? Do people really think in those moments; do they dream? Is it true that your entire life unfolds, that all your actions, both good and bad, and perhaps especially the bad, unfold in a fraction of an instant? That time as we know it – so inflexible – no longer means anything and from now on speaks its own language? Is it true that you move through a tunnel and that light shines at the end? Or that you climb into a small boat with Charon to cross the river, like the Ancients thought. People had to place a coin, an obol, in the hand of the ferryman – called "the Ferryman of the Dead" – so that he would condescend to take people across the Acheron. Or else you venture onto a bridge, the bridge to Gehenna – it is about the width of a hair – once your actions are weighed, gauged, judged. Our lives are the sum of our acts, a philosopher – which? – said so one day. No, Stefan corrects himself after a moment, no, that is not life, that is man. Man is the sum of his acts. And the person who came up with the expression was perhaps not a philosopher. Stefan no longer knows who said that. If he ever did. With some sentences, we feel as if we have always heard them.

So many legends. He would like to awaken Liri. Ask him: "Are you moving forward in the tunnel, the light, the mythical light at the end, do you see it?"

They had all thought this trip would be the last. Stefan's heart was heavy; he had almost cried on the airplane journey. Yet, when they arrived in Pisa, the old man had seemed to rejuvenate by at least twenty years. He became or again became – he must have been so in his youth – dashing. That is, in a manner of speaking. But compared to how he had been in Bulgaria as of late … he glowed, to say the least. He who had let himself waste away regained strength. He who had morosely picked at his food found his appetite had returned. The cantankerous temperament had softened as if by magic. His sharp edges had softened. He no longer croaked, he cooed. The crow had been transformed into a turtledove.

He wanted to see everything again. The major cities – Pisa, Lucca, Siena, Florence – and the hamlets. Cathedrals, palaces, museums. Four or five hundred-year-old churches, if not older. Ancient mills, abandoned wine presses. Lighthouses, also abandoned. Yuri took photos with his cell phone. In his wheelchair, Ernesto Liri was insatiable. Holding a magnifying glass, in the evenings he would settle down in front of a map to decide the next step.

They had spent the first weeks visiting, almost not stopping. Then the old musician got the urge to go to the islands. In his condition, taking the boat was far from simple, but he insisted.

Corsica was obviously too far. Stefan suggested Isola d'Elba, where Napoleon had lived in exile after his abdication. Strangely, even though he'd spent his youth in and around Pisa, Ernesto Liri had never been. So they made the journey. Disappointing in the end, despite the spectacular scenery – but all of Tuscany is spectacular, is it not? Disappointing because what remained of the dwelling place of the "big little man," as Liri used to like to call him, of his caricature of a reign – scarcely one year and the kingdom turned out to be tiny, pathetic in the wake of an empire that had covered almost all of Europe – wasn't much. They had seen the two houses, the one called *dei Mulini* because of the two mills nearby, and the villa in San Martino. And the Sedia, the rock in Colle d'Orano where the deposed emperor liked to sit to contemplate the coast of Corsica in the distance. Liri's comment in front of this rock: "What a show-off! Corsica: He was in such a hurry to leave. And to get his tribe out of there. All these profiteers transformed into kings." And in front of the mill house: "Ordinary."

"Well, personally, I'd be happy to be so ordinary," Yuri had exclaimed.

"You, perhaps, but certainly not him. Where did he live when he was in France? At Versailles?"

"I don't know," Stefan had answered. "At the Tuileries, I think."

"Versailles or the Tuileries, he lived in a castle. After his defeat, he wound up in a house like an ordinary guy."

Just before boarding the boat bringing them back to the continent, he motioned as if to sweep away Napoleon and his history. "Well, *piccolo*," he had said with a snigger. "*Sic transit gloria mundi*."

"*Piccolo*, perhaps you are being a bit unfair. Didn't he have a few good ideas?" Stefan tried to point out. "Creating Europe, for example. People still dream about it today."

Liri was not swayed. "Europe under his heel, yes. A forerunner to Hitler, if you want my opinion. The frog who wanted to make himself as big as the ox, as a writer of fables described so well. A Frenchman, in fact."

Once on the ship, he said: "He was five foot two, if that. Talk of a great man." Liri is scarcely any taller.

In the long run, these travels ended up tiring him. Even Stefan and Yuri felt dazed. After the Isle of Elba, they all agreed to stop. The last step was Marina di Pisa.

It must be said that in this village – a vacation spot about ten kilometres from Pisa that had been a seaside resort since the second half of the nineteenth century, there was Costanza. More specifically Costanza's *ribollita*. That explains the cooing mentioned earlier.

The first time she brought a stockpot full of the coveted soup – Stefan had gone all around the village explaining Liri's request as best he could (at that point his Italian had only been rudimentary), Liri, looking ecstatic, tears in his eyes, stammered from the first spoonful that he had just rediscovered the taste of his childhood. You would have thought you were hearing Proust hold forth on his legendary madeleines. Oh! That red cabbage, the firm, melt-in-your-mouth *fagioli*, herbs from the maquis, rosemary and marjoram. Fresh tomatoes, not from a can, as, alas, is too often the case nowadays – convenience is king. The *pera* tomatoes, so full of flavour, that Costanza grew in her garden. The slightly pungent olive oil making circles in the broth. His mother's soup, exactly, even better reheated the next day, as its name, *ribollita* – literally "reboiled" – indicates so well.

In short, he asked for it at every meal. And he ate it in the company of Costanza. Formerly indispensable, Stefan and Yuri were now, when the august signora was present, almost reduced to the role of witnesses. From now on it was she who brought the spoon to the mouth of the old man (he trembled too much), the glass of wine that she carefully cut with water without him protesting in the least. She would delicately dab the corners of his lips with a napkin, then rub a slice of unsalted bread with garlic, the *filone* – *"il pane sublime,"* he would exclaim correctly – tearing it up into in mouthfuls that she put between his thumb and index finger between each spoonful of soup.

Perhaps he ate too much of it.

She called Liri Maestro and the tribute gratified him. She claimed he was the glory of Tuscany. He lowered his eyes modestly – modest, him! – that was also something new – replied that others had been far more glorious than he, said that the glory of Tuscany lay with Dante, Galileo and Leonardo de Vinci. "Past glories, Maestro!" the other said with vehemence. "You are the living glory of Tuscany." A misplaced tribute, excessive to say the least. In any case, very naive. What did it matter; it was sincere. And it made Liri happy. The old crow cooed, all his feathers quivering.

What else to say except that he seemed determined to extend their stay in Marina di Pisa indefinitely. He pretended he didn't hear when Stefan alluded to returning to Bulgaria. Or he swept the suggestion away with a wave of his hand. "*Piu tardi*, Stefan. We have plenty of time." He had rented an upright piano. No one could claim that he played, no, his Parkinson's would not permit it; he was no longer a virtuoso, but he managed to stammer out a few notes sometimes, so to speak: vestiges of his past compositions, or else Chopin, short pieces, nocturnes or preludes – he was partial to the sixth, called *Raindrop*. But strangely, once at the keyboard, his hands trembled less.

He had even taken in a pregnant black cat he called Lola.

What to say except that after supper he had gotten in the habit of playing checkers with Costanza, or else she would read to him. She had suggested Moravia, but after five minutes, he began to yawn. "Please, Costanza, find something more exciting. If I'm going to fall sleep, I'd rather count sheep." While he may no longer have called anyone by the formal "lei," he was unable to bring himself to address the signora as "tu." She had therefore undertaken to read him the complete works of Juliette Evanelli, the American novelist of Italian origin and translated into Italian – vastly prolific, beginning by The *Queen of the Night*. Interminable – six hundred and twenty-eight pages in all – the hefty tome recounted the adventures of one Margot Trébuchet, a young Frenchwoman who left the depths of her native Normandy – a town called Eu – to become the queen of cancan in Dawson City.

It all unfolded during the epic and picturesque gold rush. Scheherazade would not have been able to reach the end of the saga in a thousand and one nights. And Liri, the old sultan, could hardly wait for the evening. "Come, my dear Costanza, where is our *donzella* today?" Was he really listening? Sometimes, he closed his eyes, as if lulled by the monotonous voice of his reader. Perhaps he was counting sheep. Or else long legs in fishnet stockings.

Stefan wondered if he had not fallen in love. Love has no age, as the adage goes – another claims it is blind. Go figure out what love is. Stefan had given up on it a long time ago.

The trouble began two days ago. They had watched that televised game that Liri enjoyed so much. *Il tuo giorno di gloria* – a show with truths, lies, three contestants, questions about their very private lives and one hundred thousand euros at the end. Or nothing. Stefan was far from understanding everything. But he understood the words *verità* or *bugia* that a voice which seemed to come from heaven above uttered after each answer.

Costanza watched it with them. She had just left – she lingered longer and longer, as if she would never leave – and Stefan rolled the wheelchair out onto the terrace. It was about eleven fifteen. Stefan glances at his watch. Like now, he thinks.

On the table, the carafe of vino santo, stemmed glasses, the plate of biscotti whipped up that same afternoon by Costanza.

Stefan sees the scene unfold again in his head, the last one in which Ernesto Liri was conscious. He knows already how he will describe it in his book. Yes, the scene is very alive in his mind. In the present, like all the rest of the biography. It is, he believes, more convincing that way. Closer to the truth – even though that present is untrue. The chapter is already well underway. He had begun to write it later that evening, once Liri was in bed.

***

I pour the sweet wine into two glasses; I bring one to Ernesto Liri's lips.
 "A biscotto?"

46

I know that he likes to dunk them in his wine. But he shakes his head.

"This evening, Stefan, I'm more in the mood for something salty. There's some sausage, some finocchiona ... would you go fetch some?"

"Finocchiona ... At this time of night, is that a good idea?" I ask, imitating Costanza's alarmed tone of voice.

He does not appear to grasp the irony. Or else refuses to play along.

"You know how I see wisdom: Rules are made to be broken ... And bring the pecorino as well, some olives ... I won't overdo it," he promises.

I comply. Besides, I'm hungry and also in the mood for something salty.

I return with the tray and place it on the table. Liri seems deep in gloomy thought. He scarcely budges and thanks me with an imperceptible nod. And yet I added a few slices of Parma prosciutto, an array of breadsticks in a large glass, a piece of strong gorgonzola and a few small white rolls. Even a plate of cold roasted peppers. And three cannoli filled with ricotta – more Sicilian than Tuscan – that I found in the fridge. Why not, in the end? As Liri likes to repeat, gluttony is the last sin. There's a gluttonous gleam in his eyes. Finally.

"It is not good for man to be alone," he murmurs. "Do you know who said that, Stefan?"

I think for a moment. "You're going to tell me it was God, I suppose."

"Well, yes, it was God, Stefan, the good Lord in his great wisdom. He said it when he created Eve for Adam, in the earthly paradise. Woman ... For man's great happiness... or for his ruin."

"His ruin?"

I am surprised. Liri extends his hand to the plate of sausages, reaches, trembling, for a tiny slice, brings it to his mouth, chews it slowly. Absent all of a sudden. As if a hole had opened up and he had fallen into it. I provide him with the thread he had lost.

"That is if we believe that God spoke," I say.

Now I wonder if, under Costanza's influence, the old agnostic has not rediscovered faith. Anything is possible and it seems to me I've heard of hard-core atheists who converted as the end approached. A kind of insurance for the beyond. Because he never spoke this much of God, and without the slight irreverent touch that used to make his conversations casual. No, from now on, he is serious when he mentions God.

"Of course, Stefan. Of course. If you believe ... if you believe in the good Lord ... But it doesn't matter if He said it or not. Prophets have heard it ... or thought they did. And repeated it."

"And it's poetic," I say.

"The Bible is poetic, you are right ... I learned that line in my childhood when they told us about the creation of the world. Adam and Eve, the first couple ... And I am thinking about it again. I think about it again often."

"Do you want to remarry?"

"Do you think that would be a bad idea?"

"I have no opinion."

"At my age ... No, Stefan. I am not going to ... be wed another time. Have no fear."

Do I fear? I miss Bulgaria, off course, and the thought of staying here forever is not that appealing, despite the sweet life. I do fear, perhaps. At least I dread change.

"No, Bianca, God rest her soul, would not forgive me."

Bianca, his wife, died of bone cancer in the United States. I didn't know her.

"You spoke of ruin, before," I say.

"Of ruin? I?"

"You suggested that woman may have perhaps been created for the ruin of man ... Others have said she was his future."

"Oh! His future, I don't know ... And in my case, there really is no future."

He falls silent and I'm afraid I'll see him burst into tears. That had happened occasionally, in Bulgaria, especially in recent months. Tears that spilled suddenly in the middle of a sentence and rolled down his cheeks. This is the first time here. Since we've been in Italy, I've never seen him cry.

He regains self-control. "No, Stefan, I have no future ... But it's a pretty expression. The future of man ... Who wrote that?"

"Louis Aragon, I think. Or Eluard."

"Oh! A surrealist ..." He looks dreamy. "You know, I would like to have been in Paris during the time of the surrealists. Before the war ... The first, I mean. Was it the first? I would have been too young; during the first I was a child … Anyway, immediately afterwards … Between the two wars, with the American expatriates … But while they were living it up in Europe, I was in the United States. Ironic, don't you think?"

"You were earning your living."

"I was earning my living in the United States… That's one of my regrets, Stefan. I could have gone to Paris like all those artists, you know … Hemingway and … and … "

"F. Scott Fitzgerald."

"Yes, him, Gatsby and his Zelda, a whimsical woman, so they say. And the others … I would have lived in Saint-Germain-des Prés, gone to cafés, basement nightclubs. Written songs for that beautiful singer in black … Juliette Gréco … Lived the life of a night owl … Perhaps I would have become a surrealist musician … I would have collaborated with the big names, Carné, Cocteau perhaps … I chose money and crassness. Robert Elkis."

"No regrets now. You had a fine life."

Liri shrugs his thin shoulders. An almost unbearably heady scent arises from the garden, lingers in the still air. Almost sorrowful. In the sky, the moon has shifted. Then, drawn by the smell of food, Lola the cat emerges from who knows where and approaches the table. Liri hands her a piece of ham, leans over his wheelchair to scratch her head. He remains silent.

"You seem so melancholy this evening," I say.

"Melancholy? I don't know. I was thinking of the passage of time. We are so little, Stefan … It must be because of the novel Costanza has been reading to me for a few days. The Queen of the Night, by someone called Giulietta … Giulietta Vanella, author of a string of bestsellers.

"Evanelli. An Italian American," I say.

"Do you know her?"

"The name."

"I didn't say it to Costanza; I certainly don't want to hurt her, but the novel is beginning to bore me a bit."

"Less than Moravia."

"Less than Moravia … At first, I liked it a lot, but it's very long, you see. Too long. I wonder if I'll live long enough to find out the ending … The Queen of the Night by Eva … "

"Juliette Evanelli."

"… describes the adventures of Margot … Margot something … Tribou, I think … Tribouché … Anyway … It doesn't matter. Margot, that's all … A young Frenchwoman who leaves the depths of Normandy … a city called … I don't know, you wonder where they come up with those names, as unpronounceable in Italian as in English … and becomes queen of the cancan in the Klondike."

"That's what saddens you? A queen of the cancan: I find that rather funny."

"It reminded me of a movie … Sleepless Night …"

"Sleepless Night at the Border."

"That was a long time ago … I wrote the music."

"I know," I say. "I know all your movies. In Mexico, that one, wasn't it?"

"Yes, in Mexico … in the forties."

He sighs.

"I take no pride in it, you know … I also wrote the music for bad movies. When I began, I mean. I took what I was offered, I didn't really have the choice …"

He takes another slice of finocchiona, tears it, gives half to the cat who catches it with an expert claw.

"I'm crazy about this cat. We had a Persian cat in Bianca's time … Rodolfo, a lovely cat. Neutered. But not as beautiful as you, Lola. Soon she'll have her kittens. Tonight, maybe … A matter of days. Look at her, Stefan."

"Yes," I say. "It's going to be soon."

"A matter of days," he repeats. "Four, I would say. Four kittens … When I was a child, people drowned kittens … And I cried each time. I wanted to keep them all. My father thought I was very emotional, crying over that. The sensitivity of a little girl … Needless to say, it enraged him."

He pets Lola's head. "Don't be afraid. We won't drown your babies, mia cara … Did they do that in your house too, Stefan?"

I reply that we didn't have a cat. We had a dog, a male sheepdog, a mongrel. No offspring to drown. He smiles.

"That's good."

He remains silent for a moment, points to his glass with a trembling finger. I give him a sip of wine.

"If we'd stuck to the screenplay, it could have been a good movie," he continues. "In the end, one story's as good as another, isn't it, so that one or another ... One story's as good as another ... Or else, people are always telling the same one ... Don't you think?"

"With variants," I say. "But yes, always the same story, more or less. There aren't that many possibilities in the end."

"The shooting didn't go well; half the team came down with gastroenteritis ... turista. It was so hot ... Too hot ... Too ... And that humidity ... As they say, the magic wasn't there. And the editing, afterwards, didn't help matters ... The novel Costanza was reading made me think of it again. Because the film also told the story of a dancer, Lola ... A dancer who, also, liked showing off in dives."

"Another Lola?"

"No, no, I'm wrong, Lola was in Broken Wings ... I forget the name of the dancer, it was a long time ago. Far too long ...Perhaps her name was Margot. Or Marge, Margie ..."

"Marjorie Martinez played the role of the dancer," I say to get him back on track.

"Yes, it was the same actress, Marjorie, that's why I am confused ... Marjorie Martinez ... I met her during filming. In a border town, in Mexico ... Ciudad Juarez."

I give a start.

"Ciudad Juarez, really? You never mentioned that to me. That's where all those women were murdered. A lot was said about that."

"It was quieter back then. Or else nothing was said about it ... But you're supposed to have seen all my movies; you should know the dancer's name."

"It was a long time ago for me too."

He sighs again, falls silent. I offer him half of a roll spread with cheese. He shakes his head. "Give me a biscotto instead," he says. "Dunked in wine."

He savours it with obvious pleasure. "Divine," he murmurs. "Costanza's biscotti." I agree. One reason is as good as another to fall in love.

"I didn't always go on location, of course," he continues. "But this time, I wanted to be there ... I wanted to. I was inspired by traditional Mexican music. One beautiful song in particular, La llorona ... There was a scene with mariachis."

He sings the tune to himself in his cracked voice.

"Llorona, means 'always crying'.. A beautiful song really, I remember. Very sad as well. About the Indian interpreter of the conqueror, that Spaniard ..."

"Cortés?"

"Cortés, yes. His interpreter. Anyway, that's what I was told, I think ... I'd composed variations on the theme ... And that's where I met Marjorie. Ciudad Juarez, at the American border ... Where our affair began ... The movie won't go down in history, but she will."

"You too," I say.

"Oh! Me ..."

He makes a gesture of denial. I insist: "Yes, you." But he doesn't seem to hear me.

"Those were youthful indiscretions ..." he says finally ... "Well, youthful ... I was about forty at the time. No, I didn't have the excuse of youth ... Afterwards, she landed her big role in Broken Wings. *The only big one, the one that went down in history. Because without that role, who would remember her now? People forgot her other films long ago ... And she fell in love with Bob. Bob Elkis. The immortal."*

He coughs out a little sarcastic laugh.

"She did persuade him to let me do the music, though. How she managed I don't know. Women have their secrets ... their techniques ... I wasn't well known at the time, not at all ... I had only contributed to very minor films ... Yes, I owe my glory to Marjorie."

Then: "The love of my life, I think. There is only one, you know, you meet her or you don't ... But I, I was not the love of her life."

He had never spoken of her like that. He brought her up often – in Bulgaria, almost every day, less here – but never in those terms. We reinvent the past, historians do it all the time ... How to know what he is feeling now? The black wing of death is brushing against him, perhaps. Someone is walking over his grave.

***

Yuri joined them a little bit later – it must have been about one in the morning – on the terrace. He'd been at a discotheque. They joked about his conquests while Yuri devoured the food still on the table.

"Well, what about the latest?" Liri asked.

And Yuri, tersely "Canadian."

"What's the lucky girl's name?"

"Kim."

"A pretty name," the old man said.

"And a pretty girl."

"This is Don Juan," Stefan said. "The heartbreaker. When we're back in Bulgaria, I predict that there will be a new river in Marina di Pisa. Created by all the tears of the inconsolable girls he left on its shores."

Liri turned to him. "And you, Stefan? In all these years, I've never known you to have the least little affair. You're not a monk, are you?"

"No."

Yuri burst out laughing. "Oh yes! Yes, he is."

They finished the wine. Then Liri demanded his ritual cigarette, the last of the day – he smoked three of them. The very last one, in fact. The condemned man's last cigarette. But that was something no one knew. Stefan carried the plates and glasses to the kitchen, Yuri wheeled the grandfather to his room, got him ready for the night.

And then – scarcely an hour had past, Yuri was watching the last movie on TV, Stefan was writing his account of the evening – a sort of shriek came from the old musician's room. Stefan and Yuri ran there. Pathetic retching, eyes rolled back, the poor man seemed on the verge of expiring. Yuri straightened him in his bed. They were able to stop him from choking on his vomit. Between two gasps, he said, begging: "No hospital!" The terror in his eyes. Stefan squeezed his hand. "No, no hospital," he said. "You won't go to the hospital. You'll stay here."

The doctor didn't give them much hope. In fact, he didn't give them any. Blood pressure was very low, the pulse very weak. Heart, liver, stomach, lungs: all those organs were tired. There comes a point when … "You understand me, right?" he said in a weary voice. "Trying to prolong things wouldn't make sense in his case. There comes a point when even the doctor must give up."

Stefan informed the family in the early hours of the morning. That is, he phoned Laura and the news travelled. Children – old children now – grandchildren, various spouses, great-grandchildren, nephews and nieces, all know. Laura – Liri's daughter, who lives in Pisa – arrived first, with GianCarlo, her husband – the third – and Jennifer, the beloved granddaughter, Liri's favourite grandchild. Liri had never even loved his own children as much. Laura kept repeating: "I knew it. This trip was too much for him. I'd told him," with a resentful look at Stefan, as if he were the one responsible – and perhaps he is responsible, he tells himself now. Sausage, wine, gorgonzola at midnight – Liri even ate half a cannolo. To please the old man, he had gone too far, and so he had hastened the end. GianCarlo tapped Laura on the shoulder: "He's almost a hundred years old, *mia cara*." Franco and his daughter Vickie, the unpopular one – her expression was inscrutable in the room earlier. Some have been there since yesterday, others arrived today and the last ones are expected tonight. They're coming and going like wandering souls. The priest came this afternoon, Costanza insisted, Laura as well. But Liri did not regain consciousness to regret his past sins. Only in the early evening, when his granddaughters entered the room, did he open his eyes for a fraction of an instant.

Yuri watches the soccer game with the men of the family: The Bulgarian team is playing Argentina. He doesn't want to miss a second, especially as for him the moment is almost historic – this is the first time since 1998 that the Bulgarians have qualified for the World Cup. They set up a TV outside on the terrace and don't shout too loudly. The truth is, they watch the game in silence. Who would think to reproach them? Life and death follow hand in hand and always have.

To feed everyone, Costanza made a foray to the market, then besieged the kitchen. Crying, she swore that no one could question her *ribollita*. The doctor reassured her: no, no, she should calm down. "No one is thinking of calling your soup into question, signora. You are above suspicion." More likely, a set of circumstances was to blame, he explained. "Among them, the emotion of seeing his part of the country again. And if *ribollita* must be mentioned, perhaps also the joy of finding what he had thought forever lost. The flavour of his childhood in Tuscany. In the end, you made him happy. That's all that matters."

Stefan glances at the screen. The loathsome Bromsky has just shot Stephen – his namesake – and Stephen has collapsed on the sidewalk while the killer's Daimler speeds away, disappearing in the fog. An almost elegant fall, in slow motion, hand on his chest, a black stain slowly spreading across the white shirt – the film is in black and white – in the area of the heart. That's how it is in the movies. And despite everything for which Robert Elkis can be criticized, he was unquestionably a genius at the play of shadows and light. In reality, however, death is less aesthetic.

Presently, the dying man in the room turns his head right and left on the pillow. As if he were being attacked. Stefan takes his hand. The passage is not easy, Ernesto Liri. Are you afraid? Yes, he is afraid, of course. Or else he is denying, resisting. Despite the morphine, he is still resisting. He doesn't want to let go of this life from which he claimed he was detached. Stefan holds the bony hand – the hand of a skeleton, he thinks – without knowing if the gesture brings some comfort to the dying man. We die alone.

Suddenly, a thought disturbs him. He wonders if Ernesto Liri has named him in his will. Because if not there could be hard times ahead. A base thought, of course, sordid even, and he is angry at himself for having it, especially right now. But baseness does not prevent attachment. He has become attached to Liri over the years.

Now his future seems uncertain. He thinks of the house overlooking the Black Sea; he has lived there for twelve years: It's home. The heirs will sell it surely. And where will he live after Liri's death?

Of course there is the biography – unauthorized, for which he could sell the rights when he finishes. But who would be interested? Stefan has no illusion: He won't make a fortune with the life of Ernesto Liri. His life as he lived it. He composed the song and music of an art film – and of many others as well, true, but only one achieved cult status – and won an Oscar more than a half century ago. So what? A lot of water has flowed under the bridge since the film and its statuette, and people barely remember his name.

And that doesn't make him Mozart, or Frédéric Chopin, far from it. Neither their music nor their lives are comparable. Nor their deaths. They both died young, and that gives them a romantic aura. Liri endured – in fact, he continues to endure, he's not yet dead – and longevity is unquestionably less exciting. No, Stefan understands that he will have to embellish. Who still thinks that biographies tell the truth? Certainly not Ernesto Liri. When Stefan read the life story of some celebrity to him, he always would protest, outraged, shrieking: "A web of lies! It didn't happen that way at all."

Be that as it may – and it's paradoxical – uncovering the lie delighted him. That TV show, for example, that he never wanted to miss.

The last time he'd watched it with Costanza, who'd cried out, horrified, at the indecency of certain revelations. "The lure of money," she had commented, shaking her head disapprovingly.

"No doubt," Liri had replied, "but more than that, it's nostalgia for the confessional that titillates them … Nostalgia for the confessional, believe me. They want to confess."

Stefan had shrugged his shoulders: that nostalgia, he didn't know – he has never been to confession.

"They want to free themselves of the weight of their sins," Liri had insisted.

And also: "They've given up on tradition, and look where it's led: to a TV set where they expose their perversions."

"Not only their perversions," Stefan had said. "Their failures too. Their sorrows."

It's true; some could barely hold back their tears.

But Liri, without compassion, had let out a rasping laugh when the doleful voice decreed "*Menzogna!*" "Liar!" he had gloated. Or else "He lied!" The acknowledgement delighted him.

"And their grudges, Stefan. Don't forget the grudges. Our past is filled with grudges. People do not forgive … Do you forgive?"

What did he also say? That people don't forgive, but want themselves to be forgiven. That they like suffering; deep down, suffering excites them. That of others, their own as well. They ask for more. "But they lie. They can't help themselves. It just comes out."

Yet he himself, when did he tell the truth? He mixed up dates, places, names, and it was up to Stefan to distinguish between the real and the imagined. Truth reinvents itself. It is fluid, changing, relative, never absolute; he's understood that for a long time. Now he is looking for where to place his bets.

Probably Liri crossed paths with the unforgettable Marilyn Monroe, as well as other icons, when he lived in Hollywood. No real evidence. Invited to the same parties on a few occasions. More brushed past them than really met. And even then, there's no guarantee that he even brushed past her. Stefan tried hard to elicit confidences, but Liri had little to say about the goddess. "Very beautiful; not as dazzling as in her movies, but still attractive, it's true. I remember how shy she was … Yes, in the end, that's it, she was a shy girl. And drunk most of the time … I never composed music for her movies. But there weren't all that many."

Be that as it may, Marilyn Monroe is still a safe bet and Stefan tells himself he could imagine an idyll – that no one ever mentioned – between the two. A kind of revelation that would make the book more enticing. And if someone voices doubts, he will reply that he merely repeated some of Liri's confidences. After all, what difference does it make to history if Marilyn is given another lover, she who, if you believe her biographers – them again – had too many to count. He would only be adding a flower – a crocus? the comparison makes him smile despite the seriousness of the moment – to an already full bouquet.

Marilyn, President Kennedy perhaps, and his brother the Senator. They too went to those parties; everyone went. All important people, the well-known ones.

The public loves when people in high places have defects; Stefan knows it. In a way, the fact that they too are corrupt – liars, venal, debauched – seems to reassure them. So he will embroider on the defects of the rich. Who could contradict him? When the book is published – if it is – all the protagonists will be dead and buried. No danger of them leaving their graves – even when there's a full moon – to demand truth and justice. People who aren't there get blamed. Fortunately for their biographers.

He doesn't want to be too hard on Ernesto Liri, to bite the hand that fed him for twelve years. But the others, those he came in contact with during his glory days in Hollywood?

Marjorie Martinez took drugs – nothing more commonplace nowadays. Liri's own family has not been spared; one look at Vickie's bare arms in the room earlier was proof of that. Marjorie had an abortion – commonplace as well. Robert Elkis liked the company of young girls. Very young, even. That is juicier. Stefan remembers that Liri sometimes alluded – very cryptically – to special parties in Santa Monica. Parties that Elkis and others attended, but not him. On that point, he was adamant. Not him.

These thoughts – they come in spite of himself – depress Stefan. He watches him dying, feels like an orphan all of a sudden. "Don't die," he says very softly.

Laura – or is it Franco? – is on the point of coming to replace him. He is thinking of joining the men on the terrace. He wonders if the game is over. They finish late sometimes, when the play is stopped a lot: yellow cards, red cards, players injured. Afterwards he will write, add a few sentences to the biography.

Now Lola is in front of the mirror, her lipstick in her hand. Broken Wings is about to end. Then begin again.

4

Truth and Lies on a TV Set

... in a bathtub, wrists slashed ...
... a show with truths, lies, three
contestants, questions about their very
private lives, one hundred thousand
euros at the end. Or nothing.

In the living room of the villa, Vickie, the black sheep of the family, drug addict, bipolar, chronic runaway, and Jennifer, Nini, the youngest – eighteen years old – are in front of the TV screen. The former, with her dishevelled shock of red hair, faded jeans torn at both knees, and canary yellow tank top, is sprawled on the couch. A feline – puma, panther, black in any case – showing its fangs is tattooed on her right shoulder. Seated in the wing chair, the latter wears a short dress with coral stripes on a white background, buttoned in the front. Parted in the middle, her black hair to her waist, where it hangs, perfectly even. She looks straight out of a preppy magazine on glossy paper. Vickie has a pale, angular face, and is barefoot. She is chain-smoking, lighting one cigarette from the butt of the other. Nini has softer features in an oval, almost round face – the face of a Madonna – a light tan testifying to a healthy lifestyle, and is wearing white leather sandals that look new. She doesn't smoke. Impossible to resemble each other less. They are cousins, however, the granddaughters of Ernesto Liri, now dying in the next room. The entire family – at least the ones who can, who live in Italy – will soon be reunited. For the old man's death.

They saw him earlier – not for long – one at a time, entering the room on tiptoe. He seemed to recognize them. Especially Nini, his favourite. For a fleeting moment, a ghost of a smile softened his features when she approached. But it is true that she was still fresh in his memory: She spent a week at his house on the Black Sea last winter. He doesn't know Vickie as well. And she changes; yesterday a brunette, today a redhead. She even dyed her hair green once, which her grandfather found vulgar, to say the least.

He looked at her with his glazed eyes – at least, she had the impression he looked at her. "It's Vittoria, nonno," she murmured. "Vickie." "The one you never bounced on your knee, the one you never kissed. Vickie," she could have added, but what would have been the point? So she didn't. Besides, he was not the type to make a fuss of the children; he was too busy for that, or too self-centred. Except when it came to Nini, of course. In Bulgaria, when the entire family flew in to celebrate Christmas with him. *Oh! But what do I see here?* he would chirp. *My little Nini! Come, come give Grandpa a kiss,* tesoro! But she'd been born after the others and he was already gaga.

Vickie said nothing; she wasn't going to sink into melodrama. She isn't jealous. She doesn't give a damn. She doesn't give a damn now. That's all in the past. In her childhood, it was different. Once – she must have been six or seven – she had learned the famous song in English and sung it for him in the living room in front of the assembled family. It was in Italy, that time, at her parents' home. He had not yet bought the house on the Black Sea. And *nonna* was alive. Her last Christmas. Or second to last. *Nonna* never knew the house in Bulgaria, or Jennifer, even as a baby. The grumpy old man's only comment: "That poor child is so off key." Not a word to acknowledge the effort – the superhuman effort – she'd made to sing in front of him. She doesn't give a damn now. But she doesn't forget.

Earlier, he'd looked at her with his glazed eyes; his eyelids blinked; that was all. Hard to say whether he recognized her. Or whether he was aware of her presence, whether he even remembered she existed. Whether he was still there.

Now Stefan, his secretary, is with him. All night they'll take turns at the bedside of the dying man, that is, until the end. The doctor said he probably wouldn't see the dawn; he's come to the end of the road. Laura, Jennifer's mother, is resting, waiting her turn to go on watch. Afterwards, Vickie's father, Franco, will replace her, then someone else will replace him. Vickie would like to be the one who sees him kick the bucket. Because that's a moment that fascinates her: the one when you slip away from this world to the next, whatever it may be.

Death is a spectacle; it has always been. In times gone by, executions were public and crowds rushed to them. Still today, perhaps, in some countries. She doesn't know. Lucky told her that in China, at the beginning of the last century, not so long ago, there were torture fields where people – even children – could see executioners cut criminals into a hundred pieces. Photos exist. What's more, the condemned enjoyed the torture. Their faces, apparently, bore the same expression as at the moment of orgasm. A hundred pieces, and alive until the last one, the head, probably.

She wonders if it's true. If the fact they bore that expression means something. And how a person feels after seeing that. There are things that stain the soul forever, if indeed people have one. As for the grandfather, Vickie has no illusions: She won't see much. Given all the morphine they're injecting him with, he himself is likely to pass away without catching a glimpse of the soul he has or doesn't have.

The two cousins watch television. Not much else to do. They aren't very well going to say the rosary. Vickie is drinking red wine. Her therapist recommended she stick to fruit juice as much as possible but, as she says, wine is made with grapes. And everyone claims it's very healthy, an elixir for the arteries. The Mediterranean diet: olive oil, red wine and all that – they swear only by that now. As if people on the Mediterranean don't die like in other places. People die everywhere, and more or less the same deaths. Coke too, is natural; it's made with the leaves of the coca plant, which grows in the mountains of Bolivia. The sacred plant of the Incas. And perhaps heroine is plant-based as well? The poppy. All that comes from nature and yet is forbidden. They'd like to see us all on vegetables and water.

Jennifer sips iced tea.

They don't often have the chance to see one another. Vickie is emerging from her umpteenth stint in rehab. Her slashed wrists – she displays them unashamedly with other marks no less eloquent – bear witness to her difficulties. Existential, as she describes them, a grin of derision on her lips. Jennifer wants to become an architect. She has been accepted at the University of Florence, one of the oldest and most prestigious Italian universities, founded in 1321, the year of Dante's death. She'll begin classes in the fall.

Now she feels a bit intimidated. She and Vickie are seven years apart – needless to say they didn't really play together as children. No bond exists between them. Barely a touch of the affection one could imagine between two cousins. And people say – as an aside, most of the time, and in a low voice – so many things about Vickie. Her repeated running away, the first time at age fourteen, and the most recent at twenty. Missing for months without being in touch with anyone. In the end, desperate, they hired – the grandfather paid – a private detective who, God know how, but they have their ways, found her in the Balearic Islands, delirious, extremely pale, completely lost. Apparently she was begging near the cathedral in Palma de Mallorca. And other things were said in an even lower voice: that she appeared in porno films, for example, to pay for her heroine. Perhaps she even prostituted herself, who knows? With her, anything can be expected. Especially the worst. The suicide attempt followed soon after her ignominious return with her father Franco who went to collect her. Since then, highs and lows. Especially lows.

Jennifer is therefore intimidated, flustered even. In fact, she is desperately seeking a topic of conversation to broach with Vickie. What do you ask a girl like her? "How are you?" And beneath this justified embarrassment lies perhaps a bit of envy, how to tell? The envy the wise feel toward the rebellious. Everyone longs at times – and more often than we think – to deviate from the straight and narrow. It's human; it can't be helped. The reverse is rare: No, rebels do not envy the wise. At best, they ignore them; at worst, they despise them.

Rebels and dissidents are symbols; their images appear on T-shirts, lighters, pens, caps, whatever you like. The bedroom walls of teenagers. Icons of nostalgia; heroes of dreams as old as the hills. Was not Lucifer the handsomest of angels? Women – and men as well – have been dancing with him for a long time. People say that Cain was jealous of Abel, but perhaps the opposite was true. Besides, Abel died without descendants; humanity is descended from his brother. We are all children of the murderer. There's another question that Jennifer wondered about when she was told the story: With whom did Cain have those children? With his mother Eve, the only woman in sight. There is no other answer. We are the descendants of the murderer and of incest. A shining example. She hasn't wondered about it for a long time; she knows from whom we are descended. From monkeys. It's almost as disturbing.

No, Jennifer does not want to be where she is, and that's not only because of her intimidating cousin. It's death that frightens her, death at work in the next room. The Grim Reaper in black with his skeleton's mask. She saw him earlier on the face of her grandfather, his skin like wax, the bones below. Just skin and bones, as if all the flesh had melted. Pallid as if not one drop of blood remained in his veins, as if the vampire of Death had already sucked him up. Everyone is whispering, and an oppressive smell, indefinable, floats in the house. But she was not given a choice.

Vickie sits up on the sofa, turns up the volume on the TV. "Good, it's beginning," she announces in her piercing voice.

The program is *Il tuo giorno di gloria*. As they do every evening, three contestants will try and reveal shameful parts of their past. The first now descends the spiral staircase, sits on a straight chair, legs spread. About forty, wearing a badly cut suit that's too tight. Lukewarm applause from the audience. Three family members – his mother, his wife and his mother-in-law – are before him, in the first row.

After the introductions – the contestant, a pizza chef in a Naples suburb, is called Andrea – the host explains the process and the rules of the game. There will be twenty questions in all, increasingly compromising as the game progresses. Each one is worth a thousand euros; the accumulated amount at stake each time. The very few people who reach the end of the challenge take away one hundred thousand euros; the others leave empty-handed. Jennifer has never seen this program. When she watches TV, it's almost always American TV series; detective shows and stories about girls – she's never missed an episode of *Sex in the City*.

"That's a strange idea your mother had," Vickie says. "To play *Broken Wings* continuously, while the patriarch is dying. If I were him, I'd be a bit sick of it. When people talk of him, it's always *Broken Wings, Broken Wings*. As if that's all he ever did. He composed music for other movies in his day, after all."

"Old fashioned stuff," Jennifer replies. "Historical epics and musketeers, I think. That kind of thing. You won't find them on DVD, that's for sure."

"Anyway, I'm so sick of that song. I change the station when I hear it on the radio. I'm only forced to put up with it on elevators. Not the whole thing, luckily. But even few notes are too much for me."

"I like it when Daphné sings it," Jennifer says after a moment. "The French singer, you know."

"Mmmmm … Not bad … *L'oiseau sous la plouie, régardé-lé tomber, ailés brisées,*" hums Vickie with an accent thick enough to cut with a knife. "OK, I grant you that it's not as unbearable in French. I like her voice."

"They're supposed to do a remake of the film. The director is Canadian. Did you know?"

Vickie shakes her head. "Do you really think anyone bothers to tell me what's going on in the family?"

"They found another Marjorie to play the role of Lola," Jennifer says. "Canadian as well. I forget her last name. She does the perfume add for Déesse."

Vickie says she doesn't know who that is.

"The group Netchaev will compose the music."

A gleam of interest sparks in Vickie's eyes. "I've downloaded all their songs," she says. "I adore *Love Lucifer*. It's even the ringtone on my cell phone."

In pink plastic, on the table, next to the remote control, the bottle of wine and the overflowing ashtray.

64

Have you ever masturbated naked in front of a mirror?

Jennifer bursts out laughing. "What a question!"

A few seconds of silence, then: "Yes," replies the contestant who looks down, blushing. His mother seems traumatized; his wife and the mother-in-law exchange embarrassed looks. But the audience laughs.

"And that's just the beginning," Vickie says, overexcited. "They always begin by the less aggressive ones. Wait to see what comes next."

She furiously bites her left thumb nail. The polish – black – is all chipped. What does she do, eat it?

Three other questions are asked successfully.

"It's fixed," Jennifer says. "How can they know if the guy is lying or telling the truth?"

"It's not fixed. Contestants take a lie detector test beforehand," Vickie explains. "I know; I took one. You answer three hundred questions; they choose twenty. You don't know which. It's psychologists, I think, who decide ... I applied."

Jennifer stares at her, dumbfounded.

"I hope they'll call me," Vickie says. "I know some people who'll be pretty surprised. They think they know everything about my life ... You think so, too don't say you don't."

"Certainly not everything."

It was said jokingly, but Vickie isn't even smiling. "Anyway, they'll be surprised," she says. "By my revelations."

Whatever, Jennifer thinks. We already know everything there is to know about her life. The only thing we don't know is why she wants to exhibit herself on TV.

The pizza chef is eliminated on the thirteenth question – an unlucky number. A supermarket manager replaces him on the straight chair. New jeans, white turtleneck, casual looking relaxed, tanned – evidently the shopping centre's local Don Juan.

"He's going to lie as well," Vickie states confidently. "I can tell he's two-faced. I've never seen a man win on this show ... They're all liars."

"You think women are more honest?"

Vickie shrugs her shoulders.

"The idea," she says, "is that sometimes you lie, but you don't know it. The lie detector senses it right away. Your heart beats faster, or your temperature rises a bit, you sweat – things like that. For example, when they ask him if he's ever cheated on his wife, he can't get it wrong, he answers yes and it's true. When they ask him if he loves her, he replies yes again. And the answer is no."

"Anyway, I could never do it," Jennifer says. "Reveal my private life in public. Confess my secrets."

"Because you have secrets?"

Jennifer detects scorn. That's really a bit much, she thinks. Being scorned by a junkie who's been into porn in the past, and perhaps still is. "Everyone has," she replies.

No need to masturbate in front of her mirror and have arms covered in marks. Must it really be shameful, disgraceful? Painful? If she shared her secrets with her, Vickie would make fun of her, for sure. For example, they all think she's in love with Yuri, the charmer, the blue-eyed athlete, while it's Stefan she dreams of in secret. And that is not new.

"You don't have a monopoly on secrets," she says again. More sharply this time.

Vickie drains her wine glass without answering. Then fills it again. At least she doesn't have AIDS, thinks Jennifer. She glances at her surreptitiously. Actually, maybe she does. So thin – she almost didn't recognize her earlier. And the dull red hair, the muddy, leaden complexion, the pimple growing on her chin. She thinks of the men – Yuri, her brother Bruno (her half-brother, rather) her cousins, her uncle, her stepfather – watching the soccer game on TV. She too likes soccer. But her mother asked her, more than asked her, ordered her – to not leave Vittoria, as she calls her, alone, not even for an instant. She's unpredictable, still too fragile. And above all to prevent her from drinking. As if you can prevent her from doing anything.

"Andy Warhol," Vickie is now saying. "Do you know who I'm talking about, at least?"

That condescending tone. Jennifer thinks. The name rings a bell. "Vaguely," she ends up replying.

"And you've gotten into university!"

While Vickie is a dropout – to the despair of her parents, especially since she's an only child – she is certainly no ignoramus. She reads, everything and anything, and has done so since childhood.

"In architecture," Jennifer answers back, hurt.

"Yeah … *Sic transit gloria* …"

"What?"

"Nothing, forget it." She sighs. "Andy Warhol was an American artist. He died about twenty-five years ago, of AIDS, I think. They all die of that. At least back then they died of it; today it can be treated. That's not the issue. Warhol was all the rage in the sixties. They called him the pope of pop."

Jennifer remembers now. "Posters with soup cans, right?"

"Among other things. He was gay and in love with Marilyn Monroe. He predicted that one day everyone would have their fifteen minutes of fame. On TV. That's why reality shows work so well."

Jennifer nods toward the screen. "That's not reality TV."

"That's where you're wrong. You can't get more real than that. You may not know it, but the show has different names everywhere on the planet. It was invented in Latin America, in Argentina, I think, or in Colombia, I forget where. At this very moment, hundreds of people must be admitting horrible things about their past."

Jennifer feels a bit dizzy at the thought of all those black souls being exposed at the same time.

"No," the contestant on the chair says. A few seconds, then: Bugia! decrees the doleful voice. But they did not hear the question.

Vickie rejoices. "You see?" she says with a hoot. "I told you. Eliminated."

Laura appears at the door, eyes red. "Please lower your voices, girls," she whispers. She stops dead – all her senses offended – when she notices the overflowing ashtray, ashes scattered on the table, the bottle of red wine three quarters empty in front of Vickie. She looks at her daughter sternly. Jennifer surreptitiously shrugs her shoulder. Couldn't do anything, the shrug says. Laura sighs, then, eyes still on her daughter:

"I wanted to tell you. Your father telephoned. He couldn't find a seat on a plane; he's coming by train. He'll be here very early tomorrow morning."

"OK, Mom."

Laura remains there a few seconds, as if uncertain, turns her back to move away, then changes her mind.

"Are you hungry?" she asks. "I have to stay with Dad now, but I can ask Costanza …"

"Good idea," Jennifer hurries to answer, relieved. "I'll help her."

"No, no, no, stay there," Laura says, as if incapable of contemplating leaving Vickie alone, let alone staying there one-on-one with her. "It will be simple. Costanza is a gem; she can take care of it. I don't know what we'd do without her today. Do you want some fruit, a little bread and cheese? I'll ask her to prepare a tray."

"Pasta," Vickie says, interrupting.

Laura sighs again. "Fine, pasta. I'll go talk to her."

"And coffee. Strong. I have a headache."

"She didn't say anything, but I know what she was thinking," Vickie says once Laura has left. "That I'm selfish and heartless and all that. But it really isn't my fault if I'm hungry. And I like spaghetti."

"Don't worry about my mother. She's nervous, Upset, even. It's hardly surprising."

"All that hypocrisy revolts me," Vickie says. "And what's this idea of standing guard over the dying man? *Stay with Dad*, come on! I've never heard anything so ridiculous! You die alone, you don't want anyone with you. Anyway, personally, that's what I wanted. I would never agree for someone to watch me die."

There is a question Jennifer has wanted to ask her for a long time. Since the event. The incident. "I always wondered how you were saved … Did you call someone at the last minute?"

"No, nobody. I exercised poor judgment, that's all. When you open your veins, it has to be in a warm bath. I lay down on my bed. I didn't want to be found drowned in my own blood; I thought that was too violent. I'll know for the next time … Lucky brought me to emergency when he came in at five in the morning."

Vickie rummages in her purse then leaves the room in a hurry. When she returns, she looks calmer and yet more agitated than ever. Jennifer notices a trace of white powder at the edge of her left nostril. At least she didn't shoot up.

The third contestant is a female. She sits on the chair, crosses her legs.

"Have you noticed, women always cross their legs, but men don't," Vickie says. "What does that show, do you think? Are they more modest?"

Jennifer doesn't know.

"It must be an ancient reflex. Women have always been afraid of being raped. They're protecting their sanctuary. Or their babies."

"I don't find blood baths aesthetic," Vickie says, a faraway look in her eyes, as if thinking aloud. "As if there were a way that death could be so. No, we're as ugly when we die as when we are born. Do you find a baby being born beautiful? Really being born I mean ... With secretions and all that?"

Jennifer see she has never seen secretions. Otherwise, she finds babies adorable.

On the TV, the tension seems to escalate. The contestant now has tears in her eyes. Obviously: They've just asked her if she's ever bought illegal substances – that's the euphemism they use – with the child support she receives. Not easy to admit.

"Heroine, that's over; I don't touch it anymore," Vickie says suddenly.

Jennifer raises an eyebrow: She doesn't know what to answer. Vickie has often said that, apparently. *Bugia!* she feels like shouting. Liar!

"It's because I'm pregnant," Vickie says after a moment.

"Ah!"

"You don't have to look at me like that. I'm capable of having a baby too. Anyone can. Even you."

"No, no, it's just ..." Jennifer hesitates. "Didn't you ...?" she stammers. "I thought that ..."

She thought it was finished between Vickie and Luciano – an

Argentine with a shaved head – her cousin's evil angel. Everyone calls him Lucky, but in his case, they could just as well say Lucifer. Responsible for all disasters. For almost all. Jennifer had only seen him once – a family reunion where they'd arrived together, completely plastered. They ended up throwing glasses of wine at each other's faces – the white damask tablecloth all spattered – Vickie had scratched him, he'd slapped her: It took six of them to separate the two. GianCarlo's nose was bleeding after the fight. Afterwards, they fled to the Balearic Islands; then came the suicide attempt. Learning of the breakup, the family had heaved a sigh of relief.

For Jennifer, this could be more grounds for envy. She was thirteen when those events occurred. The scene is forever imprinted in her memory. Vickie has known passion, the real thing, the kind that carries you away, devastates, that scoffs at taboos. And if Jennifer is longing for love … it's her secret … she knows perfectly well it's nothing like that. She wouldn't go begging for him in the Balearic Islands or anywhere else; she certainly wouldn't appear in porno movies, she wouldn't have those revolting marks on her arms. No, nothing like that. And yet … subservience can be tempting; sometimes people don't resist. But she doesn't know that, not yet. She hasn't lived enough to know it.

"Is that what you'd reveal? If you went on the show, I mean."

"That and other things. I've no shortage of things to reveal … Lucky isn't the father, if that's what you're asking. I'm not saying who it is. In fact, I don't know. I don't even give a damn. It's better that way. It'll be my own baby, that's it that's all … no question of termination this time."

An abortion? Jennifer hadn't known. No one had ever mentioned her cousin's abortion to her.

"How far long?" she asks.

"Three months."

"You're not showing."

Vickie lights a cigarette. "D'you want one?"

Jennifer shakes her head, then changes her mind.

"If it's a girl, I've decided to call her Nyx," Vickie says. "In Ancient Greek it means Night. What do you think of it?"

"Original."

"Nyx, the daughter of Chaos. That's very like me, don't you find?"

Jennifer chooses not to answer.

"Or like her father," Vickie says.

"You said you didn't know who he is."

"Precisely. That's what's funny. And the day she asks me who her father is, I'll answer: 'My daughter, you were sired by Chaos.'"

She drains her wine glass.

"And if it's a boy I'll call him Nyx as well. People are so stupid; they'll think it's a new diminutive of Nicola."

Now the first notes of *Love Lucifer* are sounding. Vickie grabs her candy pink cell phone. She speaks in monosyllables, her expression tense, all of a sudden. Then a flood of curses erupts. Her voice is so shrill. Not difficult to figure out who's on the line. The black angel she'd supposedly broken up with. She hangs up furiously. Now her hands are trembling. Jennifer thinks she sees tears in her eyes. But perhaps it's anger that makes them shine. Or something else that Jennifer can't manage to identify.

On TV, the verdict is in: *Bugia!*

Vickie stands up. She mutters something between her teeth – Jennifer thinks she hears "bastard." The she glances at her cousin. "I've got to go. I don't know when I'll be back. Not a word to my father."

"What am I supposed to say if they ask me questions? You know very well they will ask me."

"Anything at all. Tell them I was completely exhausted and went to bed."

She jostles Costanza who has just entered, carrying a steaming platter of spaghetti, and storms out, at the same time as the aggrieved TV contestant leaves the set. Disappointed, understandably. It was the twentieth question: a hundred thousand euros had just eluded her.

5

Poolside on Paradise Island

… her husband's adopted daughter
said dreadful things about him
on a reality TV show …
He predicted that one day everyone
would have their fifteen minutes of fame.
On TV.

Eleven floors of pink concrete on a beach dotted with pastel striped umbrellas – pink, white and yellow. Impeccable gardens, two pools, one of which is heart-shaped, three restaurants – one fancy, two casual – a piano bar, a discotheque, a theatre, a fully equipped gym, two tennis courts, a spa, a hairdresser and a souvenir shop. Massages and beauty treatments given by highly qualified staff. A golf course nearby. A casino. We're on Paradise Island and this luxury hotel is the Lady Rose. A bit farther down the same beach, her practically twin sisters are called Lady Daisy – white concrete – and Lady Mimosa – yellow – that vacationers have affectionately nicknamed the Mimi. The three complexes are part of the same whole. A concept, as they say. They resemble one another – five shining stars, all inclusive, but high end, a space reserved for children and the monitors who keep them busy all day long and even watch them at night upon request, so parents can relax (or get it on) without worrying or feeling guilty. Each has its distinctive features: The Daisy offers tennis, sailing and diving lessons; the Rose focuses on dance, retro – cha-cha, rock 'n' roll, tango – and contemporary. At the Mimi, things are calmer: tropical cooking classes, cocktail making sessions, chess club, yoga and tai chi. There is even a small bookstore, featuring detective novels mostly, usually the same ones, American and Swedish translated into about fifteen languages.

Together, the three hotels offer various excursions such as a visit to the Island of New Providence and to Nassau, the capital, deep-sea fishing early in the morning with the promise of seeing the dolphins dance – are they part of the paid staff? – moonlight cruises on a reconstructed pirate ship, with crew members dressed up as buccaneers. For all ages, for all tastes. Impossible to be bored. A show worthy of the greatest cabarets with local dancers, acrobats, jugglers and musicians is presented every evening in one of the three Ladies. The schedule of activities is posted on a board in the reception area. This evening, a masked ball will be held at the Daisy – costumes are available for those interested. There will be fireworks and unlimited champagne all night. The celebration will continue until dawn. Those with the most stamina will witness the grand finale: the sunrise over the Caribbean. They will be served breakfast. For an activity of this scope, there is of course an additional fee to pay. The price is posted on the same board.

As described in the advertising, one of the attractions is that you can travel from one lady to another as you like. All guests – even though they pay full price, there are no "clients" in these hotels – must do is wear the bracelet given to them when they arrive, a discreet ribbon whose colour indicates the home port.

Here's a typical day can look like: Say you wake up at the Lady Rose. You have breakfast, then walk for about twenty minutes on the beach – cardiovascular health is a priority here – up to the Daisy for a diving class. After lunch, a buffet – various salads, freshly caught fish, barbecued meat – you swim a few lengths in the pool, then go play a game of chess at the Mimosa. You have a drink in the garden, return to the Rose in the early evening, get dressed up, enjoy crawfish in the gourmet restaurant, watch the show, then dance until the middle of the night. For those who don't feel like walking, tricoloured minibuses shuttle back and forth between the three ladies day and night.

In one or two weeks, the staff and guests – some are loyal and return every year – form a kind of extended or reconstituted family. At least that's what they claim in their brochure.

Daphné emerges from the pool – not the heart-shaped one, the other one. It is two thirty. She is wearing a black, Olympic champion style bathing suit. Nothing could be less sexy. Her hair, which used to be blond, is now black again and very short, and no one notices her anymore. People have talked enough about the Chinese blonde. She goes unnoticed and for the moment that suits her fine. Complete anonymity. Especially since she's already spotted some Quebecers among the vacationers, as she does every week. Let's hope they aren't fans of reality TV shows, she tells herself each time. Her heartbeat speeds up when she spots them among the others; there's a lump in her throat. The risk is slight, however; for them, all Chinese people look alike. And even the Japanese, Vietnamese, Thai and Cambodians. In their eyes, it amounts to the same thing. Interchangeable. They don't see any difference. It was when she was blond that people recognized her.

There are also Americans, English Canadians and some Europeans of various ages. The only natives visible – waiters, chamber maids, cooks, gardeners, receptionists and others – are there to answer to the slightest desires of the "guests." In the end, that's how it always is in these types of hotels. The blended family exists only in advertising.

The place is practically deserted – it is scorchingly hot. The vacationers are conspicuous by their absence, all at their classes or off on excursions. Or they're choosing their costume for the big ball this evening, or napping in their air-conditioned rooms. A little farther on, a man wearing a straw hat sits at a table smoking a cigar, a newspaper open in front of him. A couple in their twenties applies sunscreen to each other. The lifeguard yawns in his chair. Then the man with the cigar leaves the premises, abandoning the newspaper on the table. Daphné goes to stretch out on a chaise longue, putting on her sunglasses.

She works at the Ladies. It's a far cry from the Geisha Bar and other dives where she used to go strip when she lived in Montreal. Here she doesn't strip. She dresses up. She plays Bloody Mary whose real name was Mary Read, a female pirate of the 1700s, in the pseudo-historic reconstitution they present on the ship every other evening.

The real Mary, Mary Jane Read, to be more precise, is part of Bahamian legend along with Anne Bonny, Bartholomew Roberts, known as the Black Baronet – he was always impeccably dressed, close shaven, a lover of classical music and credited with piracy's code of ethics – and Jack Rackham, known as Calico, who inspired a colourful pirate in the Tintin comic strip. They're all characters in the show. The presence of women makes it all a bit scandalous and licentious, titillating the clients. Those two women were, apparently, more ferocious in combat than their plundering companions, and that's saying something. And then there's that highly evocative name, Bloody Mary …

When they caught them, the pirates, back then, were hanged, that's how it was, everyone knew it and took the risk all the same. Mary Read managed to avoid the gallows because she was pregnant when they captured her. She ended her days in a dungeon, in Spanish Town. When she died, from the aftermath of a miscarriage or of yellow fever – both are plausible – she was thirty-one. Daphné knows she's not at risk of one or the other. First, she has no intention of living on through children. As for yellow fever … No case has been recorded on Paradise Island, and even if one were, she has had all the vaccinations. There remains prison, but why would she go to prison?

She knows about all kinds of trafficking that is going on here. She doesn't get involved. She has no desire to. Pure as the driven snow and determined to remain that way.

To portray her buccaneer, Daphné wears a black jacket over a white blouse with puffy sleeves, tight-fitting scarlet pants and hip boots. A large black hat adorned with an ostrich feather. It goes without saying that she is dying of the heat in her costume. A sword – harmless, made of plastic – with which she pretends to threaten the clients. For her associate Anne Bonny, it's the reverse – red jacket and hat, black pants.

The show is repetitive, the scenario reduced to its most simple expression: enactments of duels, colourful, at times earthy curses, shouted out by certain of them in two or three languages according to the nationality of the passengers aboard the ship.

It is not well paid, obviously. She has no work permit: Her salary amounts to shared tips at the end of the evening. Daphné doesn't give a damn. It was she who suggested the arrangement. She said it outright: *No need to be paid. I just want to stay.* She doesn't need money. Accommodations are provided– a tiny room near the laundry, in the basement, but it's at the Lady Rose, and she is fed – leftovers, but what's the difference? Earlier, she ate salad with rice, and pineapples for desert. In Montreal she'd have eaten more or less the same thing. She does not drink alcohol. She smokes, but very little: She limits herself to three cigarettes on weekdays, two on Sundays. A pack a week in total.

True, she'd earned ten, twenty times as much when she danced nude. She was wildly successful with her boots and her lasso. A few regulars and ardent admirers called her the Queen of Our Nights.

But the weather's always good on Paradise Island. Almost always – in summer it rains, but never all day. Back home, with the melting snow and the icy rain, basically spring and winter resembled one another like twins. She shivers just at the thought of herself with both feet in slush. And then – most important – no one knows her here. Even though the name on her passport is Daphné Laframboise, everyone calls her Mary, like her character.

She has money put away in Montreal, opened a savings account in a bank in Nassau – where she spends her days off. She saves everything she can. She knows that one day the tide may turn. She thinks that when she's had enough of playing a buccaneer she could buy a house. There are such beautiful wooden houses in all colours; she looks at them for a long time when she strolls down the streets of New Providence. The prices must be exorbitant. If not a house, she could buy a small condo and devote the rest of her life to painting butterflies. She smiles in her mind when she imagines herself with her paintbrush. You know, the solitary old woman, very dignified; the Chinese lady in a kimono. Why not? One way to end her days.

Daphné likes that Paradise Island is an old pirates' lair. At the time, the population was made up of pirates, buccaneers and looters who were called wreckers. A bit like herself: She has never looted anything, but she did cause a disaster. A bad memory she can't manage to forget.

She'd gathered information before she left – the web had provided all the material, on Bloody Mary and her confederates, in particular. The island had been discovered by the British in the late 1600s. In 1718 a former privateer, Woodes Rogers, became the first Royal Governor. The first Assembly of the Bahamas was created in 1729. *Expulsis Piratis, Restituta Commercia* was the motto it had adopted. But before becoming Paradise Island, the place was called Hog Island. Animals were bred there. The beautiful ladies are perhaps lying over a former pigsty. We are so insignificant. An observation that, curiously, reassures Daphné. She often meditates about futility. The tiny Earth turns in the immense Universe and when she visualizes immensity, Daphné feels less guilty of being what she was. Our faults, our lies, our betrayals do not and never will prevent the stars from dancing in the dark sky.

When she arrived with her prize – a week's all-inclusive vacation – she was given a room on the eleventh floor, in Wing C of the Lady Rose. A basket of fruit, three roses – the three emblematic colours – in a vase and high-quality chocolates on the pillows. A coffee maker, well-stocked minibar, hair dryer, assortment of little bottles and other trinkets in the bathroom, a soft pink bathrobe. Nothing was lacking.

She tried to figure out how to stay.

Canada, for her, was over. She never wants to return; that is settled. That page has been turned once and for all. She had a dream called China, one she had cherished since childhood. That too is over. She abandoned the dream. She will not go to China. Some people could think that she is finally happy here. They would be wrong. Happiness is not her style or her priority. But she has created a life, as they say. She built her nest with the fake pirates. For the moment. Afterwards, she will see. But not in China. The dream cost too much in the end and was never attained.

***

The place livens up a bit. Three women in colourful pareos sit down on chaises longues. Then a family, mother, father and two teenagers. Golden-blond, all four of them, built like athletes. Scandinavian, surely. Daphné hears them speaking in a language she doesn't understand. The father and his offspring jump into the pool; the mother remains beneath her umbrella with a magazine. Leaning on her cane, a woman, not particularly pretty, in a forest green shapeless dress – it looks like a bag, really – limps to a table very close to Daphné. Not the typical Ladies guest. She has been there for two or three days, but is always alone, and never takes part in activities. And so pale, whereas most of the guests proudly display their tans. The man with the cigar – he is wearing beige Bermudas from which two scrawny legs emerge, and a shirt that is also beige, opening onto a brick red torso, not too hairy – reappears. He must have gone to the bathroom. Now Daphné sees the yellow bracelet on his wrist: He is staying at the Mimi. When he notices the cripple, he stops, as if he'd had a vision. Perhaps they know one another. Yet Daphné could swear not. Then he leans over, speaks to her ... solicitously, seemingly. She acquiesces with a nod, a slightly surprised smile on her lips. He goes to fetch an ashtray, sits down at the table across from her, removes his hat. A tuft of coarse greying hair appears, hair that was visibly red in its youth. Presently, it has aged, like everything in else.

The hotel is overflowing with ravishing creatures – quite evidently unaccompanied – in sophisticated bathing suits. Just at noon, Daphné counted a good dozen of them at the buffet, picking away at their plates of salads and fruit, looking as if they were counting their calories. And he sets his heart on the gimp in forest green!

The man with the cigar. It reminds her of something all of a sudden. The face of another man, with another cigar, appears in Daphné's head.

Snatches of conversation reach her. They are speaking in English, rather laboriously, each with an accent. The woman's, Daphné recognizes easily: She is from Quebec. The man's accent is harder to place. Eastern Europe, perhaps.

"Librarian," the woman says. "I work in a library."

"Oh! A library," the other says. "I see."

"Old books," she says.

He nods his head, impressed. And that is how the misunderstanding arises: One says something, the other hears it, gives another meaning to the words. It has already been called the Babel phenomenon, I believe. The history of the world is marked by such misunderstandings. For better and often for worse, provoked by these words that resemble one another, that people call false friends. Now the man with the cigar thinks the woman in green is responsible for the old books section, perhaps in a university library, whereas she works, more humbly, in a used bookstore.

The thing is, English is not their language, neither hers or his. They use it as a necessary evil to communicate. But he obviously masters it better than she.

"I am Max," he says.

"Oh ... me, Béatrice ..."

"Glad to meet you."

Romania? Hungary? Serbia? Albania? Russia? Daphné wonders. Then she hears him say Praha. Oh! Prague, he's from the Czech Republic. Eastern Europe: She'd guessed right. He adds that he's spent a good part of his life in Vienna, where he owns a private detective agency.

"Like ... Hercule Poirot?" Béatrice, the woman in green, says. A smile lights up her unattractive face. She takes out a book from her beach bag. It's a collection of three novels by Agatha Christie translated into French. She quickly points out that this is to relax, as if she had to justify a bookseller reading such lowbrow material.

"And here you ..." She searches for the word in English, cannot come up with it. "... enquête? ... Well you know ... you are following a trail."

She slides her index finger and the thumb of her right hand along the table.

"Investigation?" The detective bursts out laughing. "Oh no. Vacation only."

He says that he has retired and come back to live in his country. Then he suggests he go fetch them something to drink.

Daphné now remembers who the man with the cigar reminds her of. A character in the movie at the Sweet Dreams last winter.

Right in the middle of a snowstorm, she and Julie had been stuck at the border – they were both nude dancers at that ugly bar, the Geisha. Their usual taxi couldn't come fetch them. Impossible to go home. They took refuge in the most pathetic motel imaginable. Sweet Dreams. One of the two E's was burnt out on the flashing neon sign. Which made it *Swet Dreams* and that was even uglier. The TV was on in the room. Daphné remembers that a man was smoking a cigar while a woman cried. A very old black-and-white movie.

It was raining in the movie, she remembers that as well. And the music. Last year, Daphné, a French punk singer, her namesake, had recorded a new version of the familiar tune. Bizarre, the way memories remain etched in your memory. It was snowing heavily in Quebec. You couldn't even see the sky. Here, on Paradise Island, the nights are filled with stars. And the moon … When she looks at it, Daphné would like to walk in the path it draws upon the sea.

They'd spent a strange night at Sweet Dreams. The night of the solstice. There seemed to be signs that they didn't know how to interpret. Premonitions. Julie was perhaps more receptive than she. True she had been agitated, worried. Every ten minutes, she picked up the phone and left a message for her guy on his voice mail, begging him to call her back. Her voice increasingly shrill as the night progressed. In the movie on TV, the girl was running in the rain; a foghorn launched a distress call. Her beloved was gunned down by the man with the cigar. Julie's beloved didn't call her back. Of course not; he was already dead in an accident that occurred on Taschereau Boulevard … Stéphane, he was called Stéphane, a painter, Julie spoke about him all the time – it even became annoying in the end. A misunderstood genius, going by what she said. If that were true, the future will tell, but it will be too late for him.

They'd met at the Geisha Bar, in fact, and Daphné had immediately found her odd. The romantic one who did it for a cause: to provide for the misunderstood artist. A vocation, no more, no less,

Sister Jenny – Jenny was her stage name. And while she was exhibiting herself without wanting to, he, the genius, was getting it on with every chick who crossed his path. Daphné would have sworn to it.

She saw Julie afterwards, once or twice. The poor girl couldn't get over it. A shadow of her former self. A real wreck. Didn't dance anymore. Worked as a waitress in a kind of dive in La Petite Patrie. Is probably still slaving away there for minimum wage. Daphné has no idea. Always teary eyed; you could barely utter the word "snow" in her presence. Or "car," "accident." "Love." Half the dictionary had become off-limits. Daphné had contemplated inviting her here, to Paradise Island, then she told herself she had better not. She didn't feel like spending the week biting her tongue each time she wanted to speak.

She is sure now that she made the right decision. With two people, things would have gone differently. Julie would have been a millstone, and she, Daphné, would not be Bloody Mary on a fake pirate ship.

When she won this trip for two – the consolation prize on a reality TV show in which she'd appeared – she realized that she really didn't have anyone with whom she could share it. Almost a way of saying she had no friends. At another time, had things had been different, perhaps she could have brought her half-sister, Fanny. The daughter of her adoptive father, the one he had with his second wife. Which makes her a doubly adoptive half sister. A quarter sister, in fact. Not even a sister at all if you are picky. Perhaps she could have brought her.

It serves no purpose to think like that, she knows perfectly well. It's useless, unhealthy even. You can't go back in time; things are the way they are and Fanny, where she is, perhaps six feet under, perhaps in the middle of a forest decomposing, eaten away at by foxes, coyotes, worms, at the bottom of a river, bound hand and foot. Nibbled away at by fish. You can't change anything. It's just that sometimes she regrets – the black wing of an evil bird brushes past her in a split second – she regrets not knowing her better. Or loving her.

Because on that same day, or same night, she doesn't know the exact moment, her half-sister went missing in Florida. Winter solstice: the cruel gods let loose, attacking from heaven, swirling with snow. From the sky or somewhere else – where do those gods hide?

Daphné imagines them sometimes, hairy, hideous, their claws, their red eyes spitting fire. Death, a large black skeleton, cape to the wind, follows them, grumbling, with his scythe. Yes, winter solstice was ill-fated, last year. A black day on the calendar.

And today is the summer solstice, she suddenly realizes with a start. She lights her second cigarette of the day.

The man with the cigar – but he's gotten rid of it – returns with something whitish in a tall stemmed glass. Rum, coconut milk and pineapple juice, recites Daphné to herself. Two cherries are speared on a pink toothpick adorned with a paper parasol. All tourists, especially when they've reached a certain age, adore piña coladas. But it is difficult to tell how old that woman is. Thirty? No, surely more than that. At least thirty-five, if not forty. Some people seem to be born weary. Even as children, they have a resigned expression that they'll retain until the end. As if they knew from the moment they were born that they have nothing to expect from life.

So a piña colada for forest green. For him, a rum and coke, simply.

Though this woman's age may be uncertain, Daphné is convinced, however, of one thing: The fairies did not run in great numbers around her cradle. No, the poor thing had not been blessed. An unbearable adolescence, she deduces, looking, uncompassionately, at the acne scars still crevassing her face.

It must be said that the man without a cigar is no Adonis either. In the end, they go well together.

Everyone is entitled to his place in paradise, apparently. An observation that would almost console Daphné had she needed to be consoled.

Here, usually, the old people who come on vacation alone are looking for very young flesh. For some, even she would have exceeded the required age. And she has just turned twenty.

She knows about the child prostitution that goes on behind closed doors. Sometimes a thought occurs to her. She wonders if Fanny didn't end up there. How? A mystery. But there, behind closed doors. A kind of impulse prompts her to go check. She resists. What goes on behind closed doors is none of her business.

***

Another impetus prompted her and this time she didn't resist. Now she is sitting across from Max, with Béatrice to her left, at the next table.

She understands that he is a detective, she begins.

Retired, he interrupts.

But when you've been a detective, you remain one, right? She always thought it was like second nature.

He nods his assent.

Well, she just wants some information. She'd like to know what they do to find missing persons.

A member of your family? he asks.

No, no. A story she was told. A girl in … in California.

California?

In San Francisco, last December. Vanished into the middle of nowhere. A friend's sister, in fact.

He sighs. Missing persons, you find one, at most two out of three. The others … There are amnesiacs, of course, but that is quite rare. The truth is some simply choose to disappear. They begin anew elsewhere, with another identity, dissatisfied with the life they'd been leading. Others are dead – he makes a quick, eloquent gesture, the edge of his hand against his throat. Béatrice shudders. So does Daphné. As for the latter – he makes another gesture, more difficult to interpret. They, often children, are not found.

"They are not found," Daphné says. Then: "She's thirteen."

When the missing person is a teenager, most of the time it's a runaway. Prompted by a disagreement with the parents, but for other reasons as well: bullying at school, love gone wrong, a desire for freedom. Drugs are often involved. There are also cases of kidnapping. He pauses, looks Daphné in the eye. He can't answer just like that, he says. He needs details to help her friend.

Details, she doesn't have.

She apologizes for disturbing them and returns to her chaise longue.

* *

"She was lying," Max says, leaning toward Béatrice. "It isn't a friend's sister." A member of her family, her own sister, he is ninety per cent sure.

"They aren't found?"

"Not always."

Even California did not ring true. He wonders why she lied.

Béatrice's eyes mist over. Because lately she has read more than her share of tragic – bloody – stories. For months, she conducted research for a man who saw himself as Dante's successor. He wrote his hell and needed information on the atrocities committed throughout the twentieth century on across the planet. She read all kinds of dreadful things for him and reported them to him once a week. Secretly in love with him. Her heart racing when she went to meet him at Café Dante or at that ugly restaurant in La Petite-Patrie.

She thought he looked like a poet. When she sees him now again in her thoughts, she tells herself that his angular features call to mind more the profile of a bird of prey. With his pallid complexion, his small eyes – a pensive look, she'd thought at the time, blinded by love, a sad and touching look – he resembled those inquisitors who used to – and still today, surely, those lowlifes live on – interrogate alleged witches in dark dungeons before sending what remained of them to be burned at the stake. Torquemada and his ilk. Always seeking evil and delighting in it.

She wonders how she could have entered into his game. She read too much for him; she can't bear it anymore. Not that she had that many illusions about the goodness of the human race. No. But she didn't know it could be that evil. She'd have rather remained ignorant of what it can become. She still has nightmares about it. That's why now she prefers stories where people poison the nasty old uncle to get hold of the inheritance. Because she doesn't believe those stories. It's a game, you just follow the clues – a hair, a bit of a charred letter in the fireplace– in the company of the brainy detective. She has come to prefer lies to the truth.

She wants Max to tell her about his most comical case. "Not bloody, please," she says.

But he replies that in the end, there is nothing really funny in his job. Tailing people: that's really how his work can be summed up. People don't realize. More tedious than anything else most of the time. Sitting in a car for hours on end, completely numb, drinking bad coffee to remain awake. Or else hidden away in a corner, rain or shine. Nothing very appealing. Often it's companies who suspect employees of stealing from them, he explains, husbands, wives – come to think of it, mostly women consult him – who suspect their spouses of cheating on them.

Human nature being what it is, he observes with disenchantment. Investigations to find flaws in the pasts of prominent politicians. And then, of course, research in the interest of the families. In short, more misery than anything else, believe me. Many stories of betrayal. He would have far preferred to replace the truth he sometimes discovered with a lie when it came time to reveal it.

A memory comes to him that she will enjoy, perhaps, he says suddenly. A woman – married, naturally – came to see him one day. Very self-assured, in her forties, well preserved thanks to plastic surgery and exercise, the type often described as a winner, he says. But with her, it wasn't her husband, it was her lover whom she suspected of being unfaithful. So he went on the hunt. Did what he discover put an end to the investigation? It was not the lover who was cheating on the married woman, but the wife of the lover who was cheating on him with the mistress' husband. The tables had been turned, as they say.

"You think it is a good story? It would make a good book?"

She shakes her head. "No," she says. It is … dépassé." The theme, she tries to explain, has been used, even overdone, in light comedies—what they call in French "théâtre de boulevard."

But now he's not sure what she's talking about. "Boulevard?" He is amazed. He's probably imagining a large urban street, the Boulevard des Capucines, Sunset Boulevard.

"French theatre," she says.

"Oh! French."

"Ancient."

"Yes. Yes. Molière."

"No. Not Molière. Sacha Guitry, for example … No important," she is resigned in the face of his loss of composure.

She has practically not touched her piña colada. "You don't like it?"

"Yes. Yes, thanks."

She hurriedly takes a sip.

"You … married?"

"Divorced," he replies. Twice. One woman in Prague, one in Vienna. A daughter with the first, a son with the second. A grandson expected in late summer. "And you … a husband?"

"Oh! no. I was never married. But you're lucky. To have children, I mean. Me, I am alone."

The ways she says it.

He asks her if she plans on going to the masked ball this evening. Looking sheepish, she points to her cane, her bandaged knee.

"I fall on the ice," she explains. "Much ice in Canada, you know … And much humidity there too. So very long to … *guérir*. Excuse me, I don't know the word for that."

He seeks it too. "Heal, I think."

"So I come here to … heal."

There's something else she doesn't tell him: the – for her exorbitant – cost of the reception. The one-week stay at the Lady Rose has eaten up all the credit on her Visa card.

He pleads his cause, says they don't have to dance. He doesn't dance either. He is moved by Béatrice. He likes plump women, and Béatrice has curves. He can make them out camouflaged beneath that kind of bag that serves as a dress, an article of clothing designed to hide rather than highlight. Slender models leave him cold. He's won over when they resemble the nudes of the Flemish school. Or of the impressionists. Some of the models. Gabrielle, for example, the naked woman lying down that Renoir painted, is his point of reference since he first saw her in an art book– he was fourteen years old – then at the Orangerie, in Paris, twenty years later. His absolute point of reference.

Let's be realistic: Béatrice doesn't even vaguely look like her. And yet … he also likes when they're fragile, and Béatrice is. Her cane, her banged-up knee, even her unfashionable dress endear her to him. Even the acne scars are touching in his eyes. He can easily see the miserable teenager, hear the jeers. He'd like to give her something, a memory of a celebration to continue her life less sadly.

"And we could see the sunrise."

An all-nighter; he's suggesting an all-nighter to her. She's tempted. There's that perfume she bought at the airport right before the plane left. *Déesse.* Goddess. An impulse. She had told herself that, going to paradise, it was exactly what she needed. She has not yet opened the bottle – so pretty, the bottle, a woman, the goddess, whom you can make out naked and perfect beneath her veils. This evening, she could wear it for the first time. She would be … she doesn't know yet … What had she replied when Dante's successor – the inquisitor – asked her what character she'd like to have been? Carmen. But well, with her knee and her cane, she's not going to come as an irresistible gypsy. A lover out of a novel, perhaps. Certainly not the Lady with the Camellias, she'd be ridiculous, but Anna Karenina, tragic and ravaged by passion, or better yet, an adulated queen – Sissi or Joséphine. Something overcomes her suddenly, a feeling she's never experienced unless it was very along ago, a sensation she'd perhaps only imagined. Joy.

"You'll be my guest," he says. "If you please."

***

Daphné looks at her watch. She still has a few hours before getting ready for the evening, a few hours to herself. The night will be long. She will remain with the "guests" until the end; she has no choice. For the moment, she's going back to swim, but not in the pool this time.

She walks along the beach. The sand is white, so white, and the water, turquoise. The sand burns the soles of her feet; she walks at the water's edge. Warm waves come and break at her toes. It is gentle. She walks at a good pace in her Olympic swimmer's bathing suit, her bag on her shoulder. Vacationers doze beneath striped umbrellas. It's so hot. She goes farther, where there are no umbrellas or vacationers.

What got into her to ask that guy questions? He didn't believe her story; that was obvious. And the other one, teary-eyed, trying to follow the conversation. She's annoyed at herself now. She who wanted to remained hidden revealed herself.

She walks without stopping.

She hadn't planned anything; she repeats that.

Because the memory is there, having taken root, an indelible stain embedded in her memory. That reality TV show during which she told horrors about her adoptive father.

And because he's still there with her, he no longer leaves her. "You ruined my life," is what he tells her. Always the same sentence. He has been saying it over and over for three months. It's like a leitmotif. She doesn't want to hear it anymore. But she hears it anyway. Only when she's dressed up as a pirate on the ship, when she brandishes her plastic sword and everyone shouts and laughs, does she finally stop hearing it.

It was not premeditated, she repeats to her father. I never promised to tell the truth. It was an act. I signed no paper. It was a performance, don't you understand? Like when I did improvs in high school. They asked us to prepare an act. One of them recited a recipe, one juggled, another sang a tacky song, accompanying himself on the guitar. We did what we wanted. My only idea was to win. A hundred thousand dollars; I don't know if you realize what that represented for me. I would have fulfilled my dream … But I never planned to say that. What I said. I'd written a text; I knew it by heart and in the end that's what came out.

And in her head, he replies: "You lied. You ruined my life."

Stop, she shouts in her head.

Hadn't planned anything. Never promised to tell the truth. Besides, truth never interested anyone. Everyone did their act. Hers came out like that, on its own, as if bursting forth from her, as if someone else had taken her voice, begun to speak through her mouth. A moment of grace. They were hanging onto my every word, holding held their breath – she felt it. Everyone believed her. Indignant. Moved to tears.

She has passed the Mimosa; the hotel is now far behind her. No tourists in sight. She spreads out her towel on the sand, lies down on her stomach, her head facing the sea. The sea stretches out like a big bed beyond the horizon.

No tourists? Yet a man with a three-day-old beard is walking, wearing a black T-shirt and pants. Daphné sees him out of the corner of an eye. Is he a tourist?

In any case, he's certainly not an employee. She knows them all, at least by sight. If he is a tourist, he's just arrived. She's never seen him before.

She was eliminated on the fifth round. There were seven; the program was called *Seventh Heaven*. After her elimination – humiliation would be more accurate – when she naively thought the sky was the limit, she had to confess. Because it wouldn't have taken much for them to put her adoptive father on trial. He'd never touched her; quite the opposite, in fact, he'd scarcely noticed her presence when she was a child. A fine scandal, really. Everyone talked about it; there were newspaper articles, call-in radio programs – for or against reality shows. And he, her father, said on television: "I went all the way to China to adopt her. Now she's ruined my life. As if I weren't suffering enough at losing Fanny." And she, they took her for a monster. Everything was said about her. Ungrateful, exaggerator, compulsive liar, pervert. Her photo on the front page of the tabloids and newspapers, excerpts of her performance shown on all the network newscasts.

So she cut her blond hair, died it black, boarded an airplane for Paradise Island – her consolation prize.

She's too hot in the sun – she should have brought a beach umbrella. She stands up and enters the sea. She swims underwater, advancing with elegant movements, lifting her head to breathe. Just cool enough, just calm enough. A turquoise bed. Delicate angel fish, their transparent bodies – the old Chinese woman draws them on silk-screens. A voice comes to her, from faraway, muffled. It is her own. She's in blue, standing in front of the mike, closing her eyes. "I am called Raspberry Scent. That's my Chinese name." Her hour of glory; she holds the audience in her hand. She improvises, tears rolling down her cheeks and they are real tears.

It happened to others, she repeats to herself, she repeats to him. Her head underwater, she wants to drown out their voices. Millions of girls have been abused, she insists, boys as well. It could have been me. They said nothing. I spoke for them. In that sense, you can say it is true. I did not lie.

6

Long Night on the
Balcony of Europe

... crouching in a corner ...

*Tailing people: really that's how
his work can be summed up.*

*... that new perfume she bought at
the airport ... Déesse.*

Almost midnight. Lying in ambush in a corner; he's been there since the middle of the evening. He'll wait all night, if necessary. He has plenty of time. Usually, at this hour, she's already home. And usually, he doesn't need to hide. He just mixes in with the passers-by and strolls very casually in front of the building. But this evening he was afraid of being noticed. Because you do get noticed when you amble along for too long. She'll show up in the end. A very good girl, his goddess.

He is Rafael Hernandez Corto, called Rafa, twenty-eight years old, soon to be twenty-nine, a native of Nieles in Granada's Alpujarra region. At age twenty, he came down to the coast to work. He's not the only one to have done that. Because over there, in terms of the future, *nada*. Uprooted, that's how he feels, for almost ten years now. He didn't really make any friends here, in Nerja. Not that he tried. No, he didn't make much effort to socialize. His mother says he's shy. He isn't. Not as much as his mother thinks. He likes solitude; he's like that, always has been. He'd rather invent his life.

He feels rootless. A plant uprooted. Or a fish out of water. The Mediterranean may well be there, but he misses the sierra's austere landscapes.

91

He misses the almond trees, the goats along the paths. The tinkling of their bells in the mountain silence. Here, there are neither goats nor almond trees. Just villas, hotels, restaurants and big buildings crammed with tourists. Palm trees.

No silence either. Always the sea, either singing, or roaring. Tonight, it's that kind of racket. Enraged. As if it were battling the rocks, determined to win. It should know that it will never win. When it finishes its big show, when it finally calms down, exhausted, it begins licking, caressing, trying to appease the beach, as if it were innocuous, although it is not; the rocks have not moved. Apparently, in the end it is triumphant. The phenomenon is called erosion. But it takes millions of years. The moon is there, round and yellow in the sky: an evil eye. He prefers when it is a crescent, a kind of crooked smile suspended over the night. It is windy now: another racket. The sky is black, the night grey. The sea raging, wind howling and shaking the palm trees. Not really a night to venture outside. Besides, there's no one left on the Balcony of Europe. Except him.

He's been following her for two weeks; he hasn't missed a day. He knows everywhere she goes; he knows at what time. He appreciates her punctuality. But tonight, oddly, she is late. That is not like her. He's already been waiting for over an hour. Usually, at ten thirty, a quarter to eleven at the latest, he sees her arrive and she's always alone. She goes home immediately after dinner. She smokes a cigarette beforehand. Maybe she's not allowed to smoke in the apartment; there are so many laws against smokers now. Even here, in Spain. Here where the word *libertad* used to have meaning – true, he didn't experience the dictatorship. If he'd experienced it, he'd know that it has no meaning. But even here, smoking has practically become an offence. Even he has practically given up. At almost four euros a pack, he really didn't have a choice. It was that or stop eating. A Canadian tourist once told him that in his country cigarettes are no longer visible in stores; they're hidden in cupboards behind the counter. Rafa asked him if that stopped people from smoking. The tourist smiled, showing him his package. "Even that doesn't stop us." On the package, you could see a cigarette and its ashes making a kind of semi-circle. A message was written; the tourist translated it for him: "Tobacco use can make you impotent."

He likes to see her smoke. It's soothing. She smokes slowly, standing, watching the sea. Clearly, she's enjoying the moment, making it last. He wonders what she is thinking about. Perhaps she's dreaming. She extinguishes the cigarette carefully beneath her foot, takes out her key from her pocket if she's wearing jeans or from her purse that she wears slung across one shoulder. Must be afraid of having it snatched. She doesn't know he is protecting her: As long as he is there, no one will snatch anything from her. She doesn't know it. The lights will remain lit for still another hour still; perhaps she is watching TV in her room or reading. Then her windows are dark and he returns home.

How does he know those are her windows? Because there's a balcony with a table and two garden chairs and he saw her several times in the morning, cup in hand. Tea or coffee, he doesn't know which. More the type to drink tea, to his mind. Or if it is coffee, very weak with a ton of milk. But he knows that's where she lives. On the fourth floor, the fourth balcony on the left. To the left of what he guesses is the elevator. Probably a studio apartment.

To fall asleep, he sometimes thinks about her. In his mind, he goes over the various events of the day, the moments he observed her without her knowing. How, on the beach in the afternoon – today was it was Calahonda – she covered herself in sunscreen with slow, efficient movements, sensual as well. How she smiled, talking on her cell phone. Today, her beach towel was canary yellow. Thanks to these images, he falls asleep, stroking himself to ecstasy. Sometimes he imagines things: He is the sultan, for example, and visits her at night, the captive in the tower, in the Alhambra.

The desire, or frenzy, was born during a TV show, *Pantera*. He never misses an episode. Hooked, as they say. The frenzy was born quickly, during an advertisement.

The super cop – he's called Dante, Dante the Jaguar – was on the trail of the psychopath when that girl burst on the scene in the middle of the investigation. He didn't immediately understand that it was an advertisement; he was completely confused. Disturbed. Dazzled.

She was walking with a spring in her step in a magazine-like setting; her hair lit the screen on fire. A redhead. Usually, those girls – supermodels – are blond, but this one had hair as red as sunset – his favourite time of day – when the horizon takes on the colour of fire. That shade of red, exactly. Fire. Surely not a natural colour, but that doesn't matter to him. She could have green or blue hair and be just as desirable in his eyes. But she's the colour of the sky when the sun sets and the sea swallows it slowly. Even better.

She was walking with big nonchalant strides, looking straight ahead of her, as if carried by the wind, as if she couldn't give a hoot about the rest of the world. Regal, this girl was regal: an infanta or a queen. Easy to imagine her in the Court of Spain at the time of Charles V, ladies-in-waiting carrying her train in the palace corridors. Sometimes she'd turn her head just a bit toward him – toward the camera, in fact, he knows perfectly well; he's not a complete idiot. But it was he that she was looking at. As if his own will came through the screen, forcing the girl to turn her head. And when she turned it like that, her red hair moved like a pendulum upon her shoulders.

She had green eyes. It must be contact lenses – he'd never seen such an intense green. Those girls have lenses in all colours to match their dresses, their bikinis and their shoes. Their hair. They change them when they want; for them everything must always match. She was wearing a white dress with thin straps; her legs were perfect when she walked in her high-heeled sandals – also white. At one point, she picked up a red diaphanous scarf as if she were going to place it around her shoulders, wrap it around her neck. She changed her mind and left it on the back of a chair. She must do the same thing with men, take, change her mind, leave them. Crouching in his corner, he feels all of a sudden like the scarf cast aside.

At one point, she put on glasses. Girls are rarely more beautiful with glasses. But she was. That is, just as beautiful. In her case, the glasses were an adornment; they enhanced her beauty. She removed them. We see that she hesitates between her accessories; she doesn't know what she wants. She opened a door, went out and in the street all the passers-by are frozen. Then, eyes half-closed, she said a word, just one, moving her lips forward as if for a kiss. She didn't say it, she sighed it, whispered it, her voice barely audible. As if confiding a secret, her first name perhaps, to the passers-by in front of her, transformed into statues. *Déesse*. *Goddess*. It was a new perfume this girl was advertising.

The word, which she of course said in French – those perfumes are always French, like champagne and other expensive, refined products. Nevertheless, he understood. Just seeing her you understood. Déesse, *diosa*. Then passers-by came back to life and began saying "déesse, déesse, déesse" over and over while she moved away then disappeared at the end of the street. Her white dress was as light as champagne, her footsteps were vanishing bubbles. Seeing her float by, he was dizzy, as if he'd had too much to drink. Which perhaps was somewhat true. He'd drunk a litre of bad wine, the kind they sell in cardboard boxes, like milk.

That vision made him lose his concentration for the rest of the show. The rest of the evening as well. The rest of the night. He could no longer focus on the plot. He missed crucial moments of the chase and his mind was elsewhere when the Jaguar finally hunted down the serial killer holed up in an abandoned factory. Of course the Jaguar arrived in time to set the terrified blond free before the maniac massacred her like all the others. But Rafa had lost his train of thought. He was left unsatisfied, frustrated.

Girls like her don't really exist – in fact, they're often invented by computer software, the magic of which transforms even the ugliest ones into beauties; he saw it in a report. Suddenly, he feels discouraged, knowing that. Everything is counterfeit, manufactured, phony. They're not real; they exist only to make you dream. You just see them on TV, never in reality.

And yet they do exist. Because two days later, he couldn't believe his eyes at first. It was morning. She was walking on the paseo, alongside the sea. The same red hair dancing, the same light gait, as if walking on a cloud. He couldn't be mistaken. If she'd had wings, she would have flown off the way gulls do when people get close. Their white flight in the blue sky. Wings rustling. And their laughter, their laughter on the coast road.

She was wearing glasses – dark glasses this time. She was walking into the sun. He wondered where she was coming from, where she was going. Was she only passing through or did she plan to stay? That's why he followed her, that first morning.

Now, he knows. He knows everything about her. Almost everything. Where she lives – an apartment hotel on the Balcony of Europe overlooking the Mediterranean – where she eats, where she buys her frills. What he doesn't know is how long she's been here or how long she'll stay. Or where she comes from, or her name. What's the difference: He calls her Diosa. It's as if he were baptizing her. The opposite of the sultan who in times past would have captured a Christian and locked her away in a tower at the Alhambra. He made her a Muslim and called her Soraya.

The first time, it was a kind of game. He'd never done that, follow a woman. It was just to see what would happen. He told himself: Maybe she'll turn around and shout: "Get lost," incensed, with her accent. If she had shouted, he'd have shrugged his shoulders, as if wondering, taking passers-by as witnesses: "What's the matter with that chick?" He'd have gone on his way. And everything would have ended there.

In the mornings, she goes to the stores. On Tuesday, for example, she walked into a lingerie shop. She stayed inside a long time. He hung about on the sidewalk across the street, pretending to examine the postcards on a display at the souvenir shop next door. In the end he bought one; he felt obliged. He didn't know who to send it to. Maybe to his parents over in Nieles, in the sierra. But what would he tell them? I have a fiancée, but she doesn't know it. Except that she's not a fiancée. The heroine of the movie being filmed in his head. Continuously. A film that begins again each time it ends.

He has plenty of time to wait for her and to follow her, now that he's unemployed. He was a waiter in a café that was forced to close due to the financial crisis, like many others, six months ago.

He couldn't see her – he wasn't going to peer in the window of a lingerie shop; he'd look like God knows what. A pervert, a sex maniac. At any rate, an unbalanced person ready to be locked up in an institution. But no need to see her to know what she was doing. She was trying on things made of lace and silk. Girls like her wear silk, cashmere in winter, always soft fabrics that slide along their soft skin. In this type of store, the least little bra, the least little G-string costs three times as much as the measly cheque he receives every month. She came out with a midnight blue bag decorated with stars that she dangled from her right arm. Inside, he imagined all kinds of alluring undergarments. He continued tailing her.

He tails her and yes, that excites him. As if they were both acting in the same TV movie, an episode in the *Pantera* series. The cat tracking its prey. Or else she's in danger and he's protecting her. It's his mission. Because although it's the same film, there are variants and he's the one who gets to decide. An interactive film. The film in which you are the hero. You are the one who determines the next scene, a scene that will lead you elsewhere, and it goes on like that endlessly. You can go back in time if you wish, repeat the scene you like as many times as you want. If he wants, he can change the time period; if he wants, he can call her Soraya. The same film, because it's always her, always him. Conqueror, sultan, super hero: him. And the prey: her, to take or protect. He'd rather protect her, but sometimes he changes roles. He's the beast and she's the giraffe, the wildebeest, the gazelle. In those cases, she may run as fast as her goddess legs can carry her; she has no chance. With one scratch he opens her throat, with his sharp teeth he devours her, taking his time. But he prefers to protect her. He's not a sadist.

He follows her like a pro; she never notices a thing. She really does move in her own world; the rest of humanity moves around her, she doesn't see it. In a way, he prefers that.

He wonders if he shouldn't try his luck in a private detective agency. He thought about it when he was eleven or twelve. Like most kids his age, who imagine a life at breakneck speed, one hand on the steering wheel of a racing car, a revolver in the other, a femme fatale wearing a low-cut dress in the passenger seat. He'd be good at that kind of work; he's sure of it now. Not at the steering wheel of a racing car. On foot. Have me tail anyone at all, I go unnoticed, just a passerby, someone in the crowd. A shadow.

Detectives often have a notebook for recording comings and goings, times, places. He doesn't need that. His notebook is in his head. That's where everything is recorded.

On Thursday morning she bought a striped orange and blue straw bag in one of those stalls on Pintada Street that sell all kinds of accessories, most of them made in China. She has money, that's for sure; she buys stuff every day, useless stuff: cigarettes, a multi-coloured polka dot umbrella. She goes out to eat. Obviously, girls like her don't cook. They don't know how.

She always eats in the same restaurant, one along the beach, the Sol y Sombra. A girl who has her routines, he likes that, this loyalty to minor things. He went in one morning last week to see if they'd hire him. Even as a dishwasher: He's sick of idleness. Idleness is fine when you are rich. When, like him, you don't have a cent, it's a total disaster. Some claim that to have time is to be rich. Perhaps for them. He'd exchange his time no matter when for one of their bank accounts, one of their safety deposit boxes where they hide their money, dirty or not.

The owner took his cell phone number, but hasn't called him yet. He doesn't have too much hope. In fact, he doesn't have any.

What happens when she goes there? He knows because he's never far away, observing her. She smiles at the boss, at the employees – they know her now. Then, she sits on the terrace looking out onto the sea, orders a glass of rosé wine to start, never more than one, then sparkling water with her meal, a salad most of the time. Once he was at a table on the same terrace, drinking a beer, not next to her, of course, but he saw her from behind, her hair tied with a blue ribbon, resting on the nape of her neck, and he was pleased. He didn't eat; he didn't have the money. With the wine, she nibbles on olives. She doesn't touch the bread. When she orders dessert, it's always a piece of fruit that she carefully peels. Girls like her watch their figure, it's inevitable. She leafs though a magazine while she eats.

Last Saturday, she bought a novel at the bookstore. He went in two minutes after her. She was in the back of the store, in the foreign literature section. He stationed himself nearby, in front of the philosophy section. She came out with a thick novel with a glossy cover, in German or in English, he doesn't know. He was happy to see she reads other things besides women's magazines. Even though he doesn't read.

Or rarely. He prefers TV. There is a book, however, that he must have read at least ten times: *The Tumultuous Life of Hernán Cortés. Hernán Cortés* the Conqueror. You don't tire of the life of a hero like him. You are transported the whole time you are reading, even afterwards. Transported into another time.

It was the first time he'd ever gotten so close to her, literally a few steps away; he almost could smell her perfume. And then he had doubts. He wasn't so sure it was her, the girl on TV. Especially as he'd seen the ad again several times. No, close up like that, he's not so sure. And when she spoke – she said thank you and goodbye to the bookseller – it wasn't the same voice. Even though in the ad she only utters one word, *Déesse*. Even though she whispers it. But it was another voice, more high-pitched. He tells himself that deep down it really doesn't matter whether it's her or not. He has chosen her.

Besides, if it were her, she wouldn't be here. Nerja is not a haunt for the jet set, actors, singers, the people you see on TV. Usually they prefer San Pedro and especially Marbella – they have their yachts and their sailboats in the marina, in Puerto Banus. Or else they go to the islands: the Canaries, the Balearic Islands. Ibiza. He's never been there. Here in June, it is mostly retired people who stay, Scandinavians, who come to the coast to escape their bad weather and will soon return to their country. The others are only stopping by, just to visit the caves and be photographed on the Balcony of Europe.

He wonders why she chose Nerja. And it's strange that she came alone. Girls like her always have loads of friends to go on vacation with. He too came alone, but it's not the same. There was nothing for him in his village, no possible future, no present; he came to work. Now there's nothing for him here either. No work, no friends, no *novia*. He's had two of them. The first one worked in the same café; she found him too sad and left him after three months. A girl who liked to live it up, who always wanted to go dancing. She no longer works in the café. She got married meanwhile and had a baby. So she doesn't really have time to live it up anymore. The second, Connie, was British, older than him. She wanted to get married and return to England. Not him.

If he returned anywhere, it would be to his mountains, near Grenada. He'd been thinking about it for some time; had almost decided. Then he saw her, and stayed. Without her, he'd already be back there. He'd have looked for work. And perhaps he would have found it, at the Alhambra, who knows, taking care of the gardens, which are so big. They definitely need staff to rake the paths, gather the fallen leaves and petals. Or he could work as a guard. He'd make sure visitors didn't break anything, and above all don't steal anything. Because he doesn't like being a waiter in a café.

His father used to say: "He doesn't have both feet on the ground. He'll never amount to anything." His mother would equivocate: "His head is full of dreams." His mother understood him. Because it's true, what exists in real life is not enough, and that's why people dream.

***

Five past one now and still no sign of the goddess. Other people entered the building, a group of Scandinavians speaking loudly and a few old people bent against the wind.

Something must be wrong. He is consumed with worry. Something has happened. But what?

Where is she? What on earth is she doing? In weather like this, no chance she'd have gone for a walk. So what? Fallen into the sea, carried away by the wind?

And this waiting has given him an appetite. What do other people do – police officers, private detectives – when they're hiding out? Don't they eat? Don't they ever have to piss? Now he's hungry. He imagines a plate with two or three slices of cured ham, good ham from the sierra, the bread drizzled with olive oil, and a beer on the side. The next time, tomorrow, he'll bring a sandwich, or dried figs and some almonds. Time will go by faster.

Usually she's on time, which is why he didn't think to bring anything to eat. He eats when he gets home, once all the lights are out at her place. But tonight, she's taking a long time. She's taking a long time while he's dying of hunger in his hideout. She's never done that to him. He's a bit angry at her. Even more than a bit. Those girls think only of themselves; they couldn't care less about the world and its misfortunes. Absurdly, his stomach growls. He doesn't even have a cigarette to help him forget his hunger.

What can she be doing? He saw her earlier, at eight thirty, when she entered the restaurant – in the evening she always eats inside. The weather was calmer then; it was midnight when the ill wind began to blow. He returned home to watch the game on TV. Even though Spain was not playing. Even though he couldn't really give a damn. Argentina against Bulgaria: What did it have to do with him? Nothing. He didn't even watch the end of the game.

He never would have thought she'd let him down. Because that's what it is, like a betrayal. Perhaps she noticed him following her. Perhaps she moved. All possibilities unfold in his mind.

Clouds are hiding the moon; it looks as if it's going to rain. That's all he needs. Because he has no umbrella, of course. What do the others do when it rains?

***

A quarter to two. He's beginning to feel stiff. He leaves his hiding place, takes a few steps on the sidewalk in front of her building. No point in going to the restaurant; at this hour it has long been closed. There are still the bars and discotheques, but she never goes to them. Perhaps she's met someone. Suddenly his heart turns at the thought of her dancing in the arms of another man. Dancing or even worse.

Unless she came home before he arrived. The window is stubbornly dark. Perhaps she's asleep. She fell asleep while he, like an idiot, watched the soccer game at home.

On the road to Grenada, there's a place called Suspiro del Moro, where the last sultan, Boabdil, cried after he was forced to surrender the Alhambra to the Catholic monarchs. On the other side of the Atlantic, the great Cortés himself cried after the disaster of the *La Noche Triste*, the night of sorrows. Tonight he feels like them, swindled, dispossessed. He's on the verge of crying.

He often thinks of the time when America was called Eldorado and even poor wretches like him could leave their mountain hamlet and board a galleon, sailing toward lands supposedly more beautiful than all Andalucía. More beautiful and more fertile. There were no laws over there: all the gold you found, you took. Gold and silver, emeralds, sapphires and rubies. When you finished waging war, they'd give you land to farm, land you could leave to your children, because in the meantime you'd married, started a family. And Indian concubines: you had as many as you wanted.

He would have followed Cortés to the end of the world; he thinks of that often. He thinks of it tonight. He thinks of the hacienda he'd have built, the horses in the stable, the orange groves, the vineyards. A cotton, rice or even tobacco plantation – that's where he's from. He wouldn't have had slaves, even if it was allowed at the time. He wouldn't have had any; he's against slavery. But servants, yes. Hundreds to farm the huge property. The most frustrating thing is that we do not choose the time period in which are born. We are almost always thrown into one that is quite unlike us.

***

Three o'clock and now it's raining. His hunger is gone, but he's cold. It's the rain that makes him cold; the rain and not moving. She won't come; that much is certain. Perhaps she went back to her country. She may have eaten quickly, then gone back to fetch her suitcase, taken a taxi to Malaga and from there a plane, train or a boat. Now she has landed God knows where, in England, in Germany; she has travelled across Africa or is farther still, in America, while, like an imbecile, he waits in the rain. He should go home. He cannot resign himself to do so.

Because there's something else, another possibility. It suddenly sends shivers down his back – and it's not the rain that makes him shiver. Killers lurk at night, at night all over the world, predators armed with chains and switch blades: they lurk all over the planet. The images come and go now in his head; he doesn't want to see them. He remembers the old dream of the hacienda, horses galloping on the fields, orange groves as far as the eye can see, branches bending beneath the weight of fruit.

But the dream is silent. The dream is muzzled, and the goddess is now gagged, bound hand and foot, naked on the cement of an abandoned factory. He does not arrive in time to set her free.

***

Four twenty; it is still raining. The sea continues its uproar. He wants a coffee. He has to go home. A full half hour of walking in the wind and the rain. But he has to go back now; he can't stay here.

He's not crazy; he's always known that one day their story would end. You can't always watch the same film; he's always known that. Even with all the variants imaginable. It's just that reality, his reality, isn't enough. He must return home. Home to Nieles, in Granada's Alpujarra region. Not very far from the Alhambra, the Tower of the Captive. There's nothing for him here.

7

Sic Transit Gloria Mundi

... characters enter and leave, plots are hatched and
are not unravelled. Time stretches out,
twists around, then unfolds;
it no longer means anything.
Her legs were perfect when she
walked in her high-heeled sandals
– also white.

He cannot hear. He is somewhere else. That is, not yet. But on his way. Toward where? Nirvana, limbo, oblivion, Gehenna: Where does this way lead?

A kind of antechamber. But no door. A corridor, a long corridor. A figure all in black over there.

A lengthy silence. Then he hears. A few notes, a voice. *Here I am, oh baby hear me sighing, broken heart.* Shut her up. She's off key; she's singing my song, I can't stand hearing my song massacred like that. *Vittoria, nonno, it's Vittoria.* Vickie in a pink dress; yes, I recognize her now. Blue hair. Or green? Bianca says she's crying. She's crying? What does she have to cry about? *You're the one who made her cry. You're the one.*

A lengthy silence in the corridor. I stagger forward. Then I hear. Deafening cries of rage. *Bastard! Bastard! Bastard!* Who's shouting like that? It sounds like a pack of rabid dogs. *Freddy.* I don't know any Freddy. *Michael, Freddy the trumpet player, Fernando.* They're yapping, shouting. Don't listen to what they're yapping about, Stefan. *Fired for a wrong note. Dismissed like a nobody.* Just one wrong note; it's one wrong note too many. *Who do you think you are, Ernesto Liri?* Be on your way.

But where am I? I don't know where I am; I don't know this place. It's grey. I move forward along a path, pushed by the wind. Staggering yes, but I move forward. Tired. The wind at my back. Stefan! Where is Stefan? Never there when I need you. My cigarette, Stefan, the last one of the day. Give me my glass of raki. Of *vino santo*. Oh, there you are. A light, you say? A light at the end. What are you talking about? There's no light. Just a pack of dogs, growling and barking. One howls that I killed him. I never killed anyone. He is playing off key. I live for music; I composed *Broken Wings*. I am Ernesto Liri, I won the Oscar for best original score. An honour, a great honour to have taken part in Robert Elkis' masterpiece. I thank the members of the Academy. Thank you. Thank you. Robert Elkis, I hate you. I've always hated you; you stole Marjorie from me. Without my music, who would remember your film? Without my music, it would have sunk into oblivion.

In Santa Monica, little girls in pink dresses. Little girls in white dresses. They are blond and dark-haired. I never went there. *Bugia.* It was Bob Elkis, not me. *Bugia, bugia.* Bob Elkis who told me about it. I don't go there. *Bugia.* Come kiss me, *tesoro*, little treasure. Take off your pretty dress. What do you say, Elkis? No older than twelve. Come, *cara.* Tell me your name. Ah! Diana. And you, Blondie, what's your name? Come, come, you as well. Both of you. Put your hand there, Lucy. Come sit on my lap.

I want my piano; I live for music. A lengthy silence in the corridor. Then I hear. Knock, knock. The sound of footsteps, such perfect legs dancing in fishnet stockings, in red high-heeled shoes. Margot Tribouché in Dawson City. No, it's Lola; it's Marjorie. She's running in the night, her heel broken. The dead baby in her arms. *Forgive me, Lola.* It's because you don't love me.

I want my piano. I want to go home. To Tuscany. I want to see the Arno, the Mediterranean again. *You can't go back. There's a war on, a war in Italy. War? Fascists are destroying the country. Stay in the United States.*

No, Daddy, you mustn't drown the cats. I want to go home. Come, Lola, *mia cara*. Come kiss Grandpa, *tesoro*. Come into my arms. I want to go to Paris with Hemingway and the others, the lost generation. A song for Juliette Gréco. I want to return to Italy. To walk in the steps of Dante, of Leonardo da Vinci. *You are the glory, the glory of Tuscany, Maestro.* Marry me, Costanza.

Another bowl of *ribollita, mamma. Fagioli*, rosemary, cabbage: even better the next day. *Do mi sol fa, mi sol do.* No, you are not a virtuoso, Ernesto. You don't play Chopin at Carnegie Hall. You lack … presence, you lack charisma. You don't have the fire. A long never-ending corridor. A figure over there; the wind billows its black cape. I hear nothing. Then I hear. A few notes. Ernesto Liri is playing Chopin's *Raindrop*. Listen to him. No one plays Chopin like him. Stefan, place a rose on my piano, a rose from Bulgaria.

A full moon watches over the garden. What garden? It's a corridor, Ernesto Liri. A corridor, a tunnel. No, no, such a gentle scent, impossibly heady, almost painful, stagnates. Costanza at thirty years old, a furtive figure in the garden, flowered skirt, barefoot, running toward … Toward what? I think of the passing of time, Costanza. I don't have the excuse of youth; no. *We're all human, Maestro. Who has nothing to be ashamed of?*

The black figure is close now. It has no face. So ugly, so ugly with its skeleton mask. No face beneath its pale mask. It comes toward me. What does it want? I want to go home, Stefan. Go back home.

Bird in the rain, just see me falling, broken wings. Lola is singing. I loved you, he wants to gasp. I love you, Lola. He has no more voice.

8

Dame de nuit in
Palma de Mallorca

Or lovers who moan, shout,
sigh, sweat, embrace in bed ...
... where does this way lead?

Palma de Mallorca, June 21
    My dear Tépha,

Today is the summer solstice, and true to my word, I'm writing you my third letter. One at each change of season, remember? I won't send it to you, of course. I'm writing to you in the beyond. Coasting along, as so to speak. Out of loyalty.

I've only known it for a few days. You ask me how I know? A message from your ... I was going to say your shrew, your damned, your harpy ... a message from Julie arrived in Seville while I was in Moravia. Manuela thought it was (finally) you, answering me. I'd spoken to her so much about you; she knows how your silence worried me. She emailed me to say the letter had arrived.

At the time, I thought so too. I even thought (how naive of me) that you were writing to tell me you were coming. I hoped that you'd finally decided to take the plunge. I asked Manuela to scan the letter and send it to me. This is what I received. "Stéphane died on December 21. Don't right ever again." (I am reproducing the grammar mistake, probably out of sheer meanness.) Signed Julie. Nine words, not one more. That makes ten with the signature. At least it was clear (though not all that much in the end). Delivered by express mail and registered. She must have suddenly realized that the date of the solstice was approaching and wanted to make sure I received the message before I wrote you a new letter – that she didn't feel like reading.

So you're dead; the mystery of your silence (you too had promised to write me at the change of seasons) is solved. I was right to worry. What I don't know is how. As you see, the message was as terse as it was scathing. A devastating disease? An accident? I don't dare, don't want to think of suicide, or murder. And Julie gave me no explanation. Mind you, I understand her: If I were her, I would have felt the same anger toward me.

You have not read my letters (but she, evidently, has), so I will sum them up. I spoke to you of my travels. In my first, I wrote you from Seville, or rather from Montejaque, in the mountains. I had met Manuela, the love of my life. She was expecting a child (who will be born this summer). I wrote my poems in a state of excitement, wild with joy. To convince you to join me, I painted in glowing colours a mob of flamenco dancers who (ripe oranges hanging from their branches) were only waiting to fall into your arms (which explains Julie's anger). In my second, I was in Corsica, in Calvi, already less enamoured, on the trail of Don Juan and two of his incarnations: Byron and Miguel de Mañara. And less excited. I wrote far less. To tell you the truth, I no longer wrote. And I no longer tried to convince you; I understood you weren't coming. I was also worried about your silence. I wondered if you were dead. Half jokingly. Or perhaps it was intuition, and deep down I knew? I wondered what you were able to see just when you … In the famous tunnel. Apparently your entire life unfolds before you in a fraction of an instant. So yes, what did you see? Is it a tunnel, a path? (Where does it lead? To limbo? To nirvana? To hell?) Or is it an abyss, a deep black hole into which you fall without ever stopping? And Death, when it arrives, does it have a black cape, a scythe, a skeleton's grimace?

This my third letter and here I am in Palma de Mallorca.

What am I doing here, you wonder, while my sweetheart is on the verge of giving birth? Perhaps at this very moment, you point out: The moon is full tonight, and you're eager to remind me that more children are born on those nights than on others. Furthermore, it's a super moon, closer to earth than ever. Is it a sign? I know that the baby is expected in late summer, which explains (without justifying it, however) my lack of zeal. But what if the baby is premature, and, fascinated, enchanted by the moon, arrives before its time? Well, yes, you're right, what would I do, what am I doing here? Would I be, am I the worst bastard on earth? Never where honour dictates me to be?

The truth is I found myself in Moravia, specifically in Brno (for a literary festival where I was invited to represent Canada; I told you about that as well) when the tragic message arrived. You can imagine how shocked I was by the news of your death. So much so that I didn't have the heart to go back. To Seville, I mean. I was still surfing the web looking for a plane ticket when I came across this bargain. A one-way fare to Palma for a song. In Europe there are small dot-com companies (very short-lived, no doubt) that haul you to just about anywhere in their old crates for almost nothing. Less expensive than a bus or a train. So I said to myself: Why not? In the footsteps of Chopin and Sand.

Rest assured, I am not the worst bastard on earth; I won't stay here too long. Just time to visit the Valldemossa Charterhouse where the lovers spent a hellish winter in 1838-1839 – the poor guy, as sick as a dog, spitting bucketfuls of blood. "My cell is the shape of a tall coffin," he wrote. "There would still be silence." All the same, he composed two preludes (one is called *The Raindrop*), a polonaise and I don't know what else. When I see the cell in question, but not the buckets of contaminated blood, I'll return to Seville. Like the gentleman, lover, and caring father-to-be I am despite appearances.

I arrived this afternoon. The sky was a pitiless blue. It was forty degrees. In the shade, let me add. To think that when Sand and Chopin were there (so that the latter could regain his health), it rained constantly. That heat discouraged me, once again. I rented the first affordable room I found, in a family-run pension right in the middle of the old quarter, La Lonja, one kilometre from the sea.

The pension, the *hostal*, is called La Dama de noche. Night-blooming jasmine: the name of a mysterious flower that only opens, only releases its perfume once night has fallen. And what perfume! My window overlooks the garden. Earlier, an intense whiff, so intense, filled my room. The enchantment lasted a few seconds; nothing lasts. I don't know why (that's untrue; I know perfectly why), but I almost burst into tears.

Here I am again. I'd begun this letter in my room, drinking a glass of Moscatel and determined to finish the bottle. (If I seem a bit confused, it's because it was the second bottle of the evening that I opened, the first was an acrid red that practically burned the roof of my mouth, downed while nibbling on olives and bread. My dinner.) Earlier, I'd turned on the TV. A show called *Tu día de gloria*, where people come talk about their dull lives in front of the camera. I couldn't stomach it for very long. It was then, when I turned it off and began writing to you, that the racket began.

The walls are so thin. The walls have ears. You'll tell me that at forty euros a night (in high season) what can you expect? The walls are thin and my neighbours too noisy. He hollers: "Eva! Oooooh! Eeeeeva! Aaaaah!" loud enough to make the walls shake, while she answers, growling like a dying cat – without growling his name, however. What is he doing to her, dear God? Is he torturing her or what? In the end, when the animal inside us expresses itself, it's anything but pretty. You don't think of it when you're in the heat of the action. From now on, I'll gag us: she (whoever she is) and myself, for our lovemaking.

"Eeeeeva!" The only word I managed to catch among the panting, grunting, moaning and other expressions of passion. After about fifteen minutes of this cacophony, I took the bottle, the notebook, the pen and cigarettes and went down to the garden. It is now two o'clock in the morning.

I can hear the sounds of celebration coming from the street. A celebration of which I am not a part. Tonight, I don't see myself partying; tonight is reserved for you. Until I roll under the table; that will remind me of our barhopping. Not that I ever rolled under a table. When we partied together, it was always you who collapsed, and I who had to pick you up. Or console you. Do you remember? When you drank, you always became more depressed than I did.

But what was I telling you before these digressions? That I almost burst into tears and didn't (or did) know why … Ohhhhh … another whiff. The night blooming jasmine is on fire. The moon is full; I told you. My God, tonight the moon looks like an eye that has been watching me since the dawn of time. Is it you watching me? Have you been reincarnated in the moon? I see you, a wandering soul. Yes, it's your outline I recognize, on the Sea of Tranquility. But I'm babbling.

It's because I'm still not facing the facts. No matter how much I read and reread these terse, harsh words (I don't read the signature), it's as if I can't get them into my head. I don't believe them. I create scenarios: Perhaps you left Julie (on December 21) and that's what she means when she says you are dead. You are dead to her. She opened my letters, read the offensive comments (intended solely for you) about her, saw the effort I was making to draw you far away from her. Is it plausible? No. We're not in a novel by … George Sand, for instance (even though I admit I've never read one), or Alexander Dumas (I read *The Count of Monte Cristo* when I was eleven). But it's easy to imagine.

In my other letters, the first one especially, I was enthusiastic. Today, it's as if the excitement has died. Along with you, no doubt. Anyway, I'm writing you. As if I were speaking to you. You will hear me wherever you are. (Am I becoming a mystic?)

Well … speaking of mysticism, I now have a vision. A woman all in white (but is it a woman? Or an angel, a demon, a ghost? Yours, like in *Hamlet*?) has just appeared in the garden. She's taken a place at the next table (there are three, in white wrought iron, with glass tops – the garden is very small), set down a book and a bottle … of water, I think (we are lit only by the moon). I leave you, just long enough to uncover the mystery of the apparition. And to offer her a glass of Moscatel. More comforting than a bottle of water, albeit spring water: Even a ghost (if it is a ghost) would agree.

... I am back (please excuse all these interruptions). The mystery has been cleared up, and I still feel dazed. The apparition, you guessed it, was a woman. A woman in the flesh, an American from Providence, Rhode Island. She works at the university library there. She is about forty, has black hair, wears glasses with black frames and her name is Eva (rest assured, not the one who exulted or moaned, depending on the tactics used by her partner in fornication). She arrived this afternoon (like me) but didn't feel like taking in the scenery. The heat, no doubt (like me, I thought, but wait: That wasn't it.) She too had been driven from her bed by the racket our next-door neighbours were making. As she told me, it gave her an odd feeling to hear her name screeched like that. Her name screeched in the night. She also said (I quote from memory): "I didn't see the lovers who were moaning and shouting in the room next door, but I can imagine them. In their early twenties, probably. They make love so enthusiastically. And with, but perhaps I am mistaken, a kind of awkwardness. Touching. The touching awkwardness of young lovers." I was speechless. It was she who was touching.

It is five o'clock and the sun is coming up. The sky is now soft pink. The last revellers are returning to the fold. I didn't roll under the table. I've completely sobered up. I've never been so clear-headed. Or on the other hand, perhaps I've never been less so. I'll try to explain.

She accepted the Moscatel; one glass only, of which she drank only half, sipping moderately, while I, you know me, downed the rest of the bottle. I also smoked an incalculable number of cigarettes without asking her if it bothered her (we were outside, after all), but she didn't flinch. Usually, I'm more civilized. No, that's not true, I'm not. She didn't smoke.

I know it's a small world; we've been told so time and again, in every possible way, that our paths are filled with coincidences, both marvellous and disturbing. I know all that, but I never expected such confidences. I don't know what provoked them. Maybe the moon. The night-blooming jasmine and its scent. A few sips of sweet wine. I don't know, Tépha. All those answers, perhaps. Or because she didn't know me (it's easier with a stranger), because she knew she wouldn't see me again. These kinds of scenes must occur in the novels of the two authors mentioned above.

Where to start?

At the beginning. I wanted to know if this was a woman or an apparition. So I approached with my bottle of Moscatel and spoke to her in Spanish. She could barely put a few words together. French: useless to even try. (You have travel outside the French-speaking world to understand: Our language is an endangered species, Tépha.) We continued in English. I offered her wine and she accepted. I returned to my room to find another glass. The two lovers, indefatigable, apparently, were still going at it. They take their time to reach ecstasy! Unless we're talking about multiple orgasms. Non-smokers no doubt. Or he was, at least. (You know the message on our cigarette packs? "Smoking causes impotence." That really made us laugh. We always chose those packs, with the poor cigarette incapable of getting an erection.)

I returned to the garden; she was reading. And what do you think she was reading? Byron! Yes, she was reading *Don Juan*.

I told her about my translation endeavours (I told you in my last letter that I was trying to translate *Don Juan*); she was surprised. She thought people didn't read him anymore, especially in French. I insisted: I read in English. I tried in French: It was unreadable. She told me that reading it relaxes her.

Then we talked about travel; what I'm doing here. I told her about the writing grant graciously awarded to me by the helpful Ministère de la Culture and all that. She told me she has a penchant for islands, and always has. As a child, she came up with the idea of visiting all islands on the planet. This year she's opted for Mallorca, the largest of the Balearic Islands. She also has been to Sicily, Hydra, Crete and who knows where else. The Marquesas, the Isle of Man, Iceland. Newfoundland. Corsica. Always islands.

I interrupted her. I told her that I too had been to Corsica. Calvi. She replied that it was there, for the first time, that she read the name of Miguel de Mañara. A book borrowed from the library described his story. Or his legend. Another coincidence.

I also told you about that: Mañara, the man who wanted to be Don Juan, who tried to seduce his half-sister in Calvi, then repented. He became a Brother of Charity in Seville and devoted the rest of his life to caring for the poor, to take the condemned down from their gallows to give them a burial. I told you how impressed I was by the character (Montejaque, from where I wrote you my first letter, was the small city where he had his summer palace). She too was impressed. Wait till you find out just how much.

When she returned from Calvi, she began corresponding with a psychopath condemned to death in Florida. She went to see him once in prison. A Ruddy Wallace. I really don't know who he is, but in the United States (and in other places as well) serial killers seem to be nothing out of the ordinary: You can't remember all their names. One among so many others; I hadn't remembered his. He was one of the worst, she told me. He'd killed about fifteen children. Cruelly. He called himself Thot: You see the kind of individual. A man's body with the head of an ibis; controller of lunar cycles, the keeper of time in Egyptian Antiquity. (He was also the inventor of writing!)

They corresponded for almost three years; then she decided to marry him before he was executed. You read correctly. I forgot to tell you that she's divorced, and has two children who are twins. (I also forgot that you won't read my letter. Unless you're now reading it over my shoulder, from the moon, in the company of Thot). She lost custody of her children, naturally. At the university, she's now seen as a pariah. No one speaks to her or goes near her. Out of fear of being contaminated.

But why, why, why? I wanted to know. "A gesture of compassion," she told me, simply. "Like Miguel de Mañara." Compassion? That guy had no compassion for the children he killed. "Exactly. It was to put things right. A gesture of redemption."

Well, Tépha, I no longer knew what to say. And the night-blooming jasmine continued to perfume the air: It was unbearable. Unbearably sad.

There was another question I was dying to ask. I didn't dare, then asked it anyway. Even though I felt like a terrible voyeur by asking it. She answered no: The marriage was not consummated.

It was a symbolic gesture. She never had any intention of … She stopped there. Of sinking that low, I finished in my head.

He was executed this morning at the Florida State Prison. She wondered if he'd suffered, suffered a lot, suffered a long time. Hard to know what she felt when she told me that. You could see she was hoping that he hadn't. But I am not sure.

She told me that she left her room because she couldn't stand listening to Eva moan anymore. "She was moaning as if … As if Ruddy Wallace were … I knew, I knew only too well what he put them through before killing them. The moaning brought the images back."

The bottle of Moscatel was empty; her glass was still half full. I took her hand and we remained there, not moving, not speaking. Actually, no: That's now how it happened. (Why must I always invent?) She took my hand and we remained there. As if it were I who needed to be consoled. It was.

I didn't speak to her of you.

She told me that tomorrow she's going to move. She'll go to another neighbourhood, to the port. There she'll be able to hear the water, and perhaps, from her balcony, if she has one, see the cathedral whose reflection shimmers on the sea. She saw it this afternoon, saw its reflection on the water. To see such grandeur is a comfort, she told me.

I couldn't do it. I can't. Make the link between this woman, a librarian, you see, mother of two teenagers, rather preppy, in the end, with her white dress and black-framed glasses, between this ordinary woman and the one who'd married a serial killer. Which was the real one? I told myself: "Stop drinking, François." (Fortunately the bottle was empty.) "Stop drinking. That's how it begins, then without warning you find yourself babbling." I told myself: "She is making it up, inventing. No woman would marry a monster like him." No sensible woman. There are women who marry condemned people, I know. But a monster? One who tortures children? And she, a mother? It didn't add up. I told myself: "One of the two is fake." But which? The librarian in the white dress and glasses, or the one hiding beneath? Or vice versa. The librarian is beneath.

In the end, she looked up at the house: The windows were dark. She said: "I imagine they're sleeping now. The clumsy lovers. I too will sleep a bit, I think."

Then she arose. It was as if the other, the real one or the fake one, did not exist. All that remained was a cultured librarian, rather sensible, who spent her vacation on one island or another. The other, the tortured one, had disappeared. Just before leaving, she said: "A man is the sum of his actions." I replied: "*L'homme est la somme de ses actes.*" André Malraux. She exclaimed: "Oh! I thought it was Gandhi. The Mahatma." And I: "No, André Malraux in *La condition humaine.*" And she: "I'll check. That sentence has been going around in my mind for a few days."

I, too, will check. Even if it means rereading *La condition humaine.* Even if I find the sentence, it won't prove anything. Perhaps they both wrote the same thing.

Day has broken: It's time to put an end to the letter I won't send you.

I will go get my backpack. Perhaps I'll find a bistro already open (or not yet closed). I'll have a cup of coffee or even two. Then I'll see how I can reach Valldemossa. After I've seen the charterhouse, I'll return to Seville and await the birth of my child.

So farewell (as that is the accepted way of saying it). Farewell, Tépha.

Your friend forever, in this world and the next,

François

9

Last Act in the Opera District

A terrorist attack killed about
twenty people in Paris.
... I now have a vision.

For me, passion was all that mattered. I lived only for that.
No. That doesn't work at all. It's ridiculous; completely pretentious. If he heard that sentence in a play the author would be forever discredited.

To begin with, why would Lili say that? No, no, no: Lili is not a passionate person at all. She is calculating, cunning, manipulative, whatever you like — he has not been kind to her — but certainly not passionate. It should be he who delivers the line. Or stammers it out, sighs it, spits it out, shouts it. But it's his; the line belongs to him. He's the passionate one in this story. He, that is, his character. He called him Hermann, a name he himself could have carried with style if his parents hadn't hit upon the rather trite idea in his opinion of naming him Andrew – Andy. For Andy Warhol, his mother told him, a man who, in his day, rebelled against banality.

But in what tone of voice would he say the line? In the end, it's a detail. He'll discuss it later with the director. When there is a director. Details are slowing him down even though there isn't much time left.

In any case, he – Hermann – would deliver the line, unquestionably *I lived only for that!!!* With three exclamation marks.

He sends his pen flying. Then he looks for it on all fours beneath the bed – it's a platinum-plated Montblanc in the "La vie de Bohème" collection, after all – and retrieves it along with a dust bunny. It must be said that the housekeeping in this hotel leaves a lot to be desired. He plans to say something about it at the front desk. Without provoking the staff, however. Parisians are touchy, even and sometimes especially those working in the service industry. You always have to handle them with at least three pairs of kid gloves.

He even thought he noticed a *cucaracha* in the bathroom, the other night. Like in Mexico last winter. But not as big, of course – the Mexican ones are impressive. Perhaps it was another kind of insect. He said nothing. Besides, he hasn't seen any more of them. All the same, a Montblanc in the dust … OK, to start with, he should never have sent it flying like that, he reprimands himself silently. He has to learn to control himself better. Those knick-knacks are worth a fortune. Myriam gave it to him at the airport just before he left. "Nothing is too fine when it comes to writing your masterpiece," she murmured knowingly, handing him the case tied with a ribbon.

Andy N. (for Newman, but most of the time he prefers to say it's for *Never Mind*) Bloch has been in Paris for just over a month. Officially, it's to write. Unofficially as well. A play. He hadn't realized the task would be so arduous. Theatre is all he knows, however: He's been a critic, and a very critical one, at *Big Apple Scene* for six years. Without really regretting it, he now thinks sometimes he was too harsh on the authors he panned.

And all the elements are there. The three main characters: Hermann, Lili, Alex – the eternal triangle has always been a safe bet; no need to complicate the issue. And there's the trigger – betrayal, another safe bet – plus the torrid, scandalous, even shocking side of the triangle: Everyone always asks for more of that, himself included. A wonderful topic; no doubt about it. Glorious. And completely original. No one has ever tackled it before, he's almost sure. Almost, because there's of course old Oedipus and his mother: no escaping them. The Ancients talked about everything. Incest, adultery, betrayal, injustice –

just think of poor Sisyphus, punished for having given us fire. Come to think of it, was it Sisyphus or Prometheus? All of a sudden, he has his doubts. In any case, one or the other was subject to an undeserved and disproportionate punishment. When you've read Homer and his ilk, there's not much else to invent. Even if you haven't read them, in fact. Because everyone knows their stories and their myths. But for Oedipus, it was different. It was involuntary incest; famous, inescapable fate. Andy's story has nothing to do with fate.

Almost as well, because if we've already seen the father seduce the son's wife, the mother steal the daughter's lover, we have never, he believes, seen the mother take the son's lover. He knows he is onto something good.

So everything is there, but not him, so to speak. That is, today. Yet he turned out the first two acts without wasting any time. He's stumbling over the third and final one. He can no longer makes his characters speak. Have them speak naturally. He almost makes them sound like – that would be the last straw – like those of … what's her name, that crummy novelist? He can't think of the name. Eva something. Evanelli, that's it, Juliette Evanelli, author of a half-dozen tremendous historical volumes, the shortest of which is five hundred and forty-three pages, who, as if that were not enough, recently sought to hold sway in the theatre as well. The *I loved her; I loved only her,* that she put in the mouth of Professor Moriarty in her first – and hopefully last – platitude, *Moriarty and the Duchess.*

In any case, his review put her in her place. A savage attack – to say the least – as was her due. An execution would be more accurate – the death penalty, like in the good old days. He, known to be nasty, had never been that vicious. His review was brilliant, ornate – worthy of an anthology. Nothing was spared, except for the ostrich feather on the duchess' hat, if that. The conclusion was, in fact, conceived as a coup de grâce: *I would feel bad if I signed off without congratulating the costume designer: the ratite feather placed on the duchess' absurd headgear seemed to be on the verge of flying off each time she nodded her head even slightly. The great and sole success of this flop!* Wham!

119

In the old days, after an article like that the author would send you his seconds. It had happened; he read it recently in a book he found on the banks of the Seine, an old yellowed book written by the son of Alphonse Daudet and filled with names that he saw for the first time. He'd never even heard of the Daudets, neither father nor son. Yet these people had been illustrious in their time. Sunk into complete oblivion today. He imagines a grey, gloomy place where the souls of the forgotten mope. Oblivion. *Sic transit gloria*, as they say. Correctly, alas.

He mustn't let himself get depressed by the realization: Some – Proust, Dante, Mozart, Shakespeare – remain and he'll be among that fraternity. Even if he writes only this play. He bursts out laughing at the thought of him at dawn in a meadow with the queen of melodrama, their pistols in hand. Or their rapiers. Their crossbows? And why not their blowpipes? She would aim for the heart, naturally, like any self-respecting writer of tragedies. Whereas he… Knowing him, he would hesitate between two targets: the corseted stomach and the swollen head of the person opposite him.

Be that as it may, in a way, writing his article – his all-out attack, in which he did not spare the young actress who, very half-heartedly in his opinion, portrayed the duchess, a woman who was nevertheless flamboyant if what they say about her is true – had done him good, that night. Only in one way. Because he had another topic on his mind, to say the least. But, well, to give credit where credit is due: That's where it all began. That is, that without *Moriarty and the Duchess of Devonshire* by Signora Evanelli – how could he have forgotten her name earlier? – which he went to see with his mother Myriam – Mimi – he wouldn't be in Paris today. Right in the Latin Quarter.

Here are the crude hard facts. He was leaving the premiere with Mimi. It was drizzling, the weather almost as awful as the heap of implausibilities he had just endured for almost two and a half hours – and what's more, it was very poorly acted. At intermission, he'd drunk a whiskey and that hadn't helped matters. He nearly died of thirst during the hour of torture that remained. In short, he was in a really bad mood.

Fortunately, a gourmet dinner awaited him. A ritual between his mother and him, these private dinners after the theatre: They never departed from them. One good turn deserves another. He took care of the reservation; she paid the bill with her credit card. This time, he'd set his heart on a French restaurant, Chez Marcel, no less. An excellent dinner, in fact, he remembers, washed down with high quality wines recommended by Bruno, the impeccable waiter, French as well, but totally charming – as they are once out of Paris. He'd eaten ostrich. With Mimi, the conversation was, as usual, sparkling. Until then, everything – except the play, of course – had gone well. An exquisite end to the evening.

Once the coffee was drunk, he was sensibly planning to go home and write his article; perhaps he'd even have been less ruthless than he was, who knows. But then he noticed Iouri near the door. Iouri Tchernenko, an adorable Russian, slender and blond, and who rolled his R's divinely when he spoke English. Velvet. As if he were purring, really. When he heard it, Andy thought of a lovely cat having eaten its fill, lying in a ball near a fire. Iouri: the object of his most wild desires, as he'd confided to Mimi a little earlier in the evening. Desires that he hoped to fulfil one day or another. And the traitor, his own mother, just by batting her eyelashes, had crushed all his plans, blown out his candle. Unbelievable. She'd left in a taxi with Iouri, while he, head and tail down, still dazed, his ego in tatters, walked home alone. Those are the crude hard facts.

The good news, because there is some: That night, while walking, sheltered beneath his umbrella, he decided to write his novel – because at first that was what he'd intended to write. As he walked, and later, after appeasing his rage at the insufferable Evanelli, her pathetic play and her poor actors. He hadn't slept all night. In the morning, his decision was made. Irrevocable.

He already had the title: *In Search of Lost Paradise*, in honour of his favourite writer, Marcel Proust. The inspiration had come to him at the end of the dinner. That was of course before the betrayal, and the work envisaged at that moment would have been completely different. It was almost an homage to his mother that he planned on writing. He had even implied, joking, that he planned to raise her muffins and latkes to rank with Tante Léonie's illustrious madeleines.

After a few unsuccessful attempts, two or three failed beginnings, the novel became a three-act play with Paris as its backdrop. And the title was unsuitable – because there was definitely nothing Proustian about the story. Never would Jeanne Proust, the very embodiment of unconditional maternal love, have dreamed of scorning her son's feelings with such thoughtlessness. In any case, it was a title for a novel; simply inconceivable for a play. Andy will find another title. It's well known that some authors only find their titles at the end, once the work is written. He'll be like them.

In the beginning, for the setting, he'd hesitated. The Actors Studio in the fifties appealed to him. He planned to use Paula Strasberg for inspiration in creating Lili, elaborating on her twisted relationship with Marilyn Monroe – and Monroe's dependency on Strasberg. And for the occasion Marilyn would have become a promising young, neurotic actor – Jimmy Dean? Marlon Brando? Max or Alex – he hesitated – Delmonico. He also thought of Hollywood in the same years with the same protagonists more or less.

In the end, Paris won out. The interwar years were such a fertile time in Saint-Germain-des Prés.

He'd been thinking about it for a long time, writing, without ever taking the plunge – an attack of nerves, quite understandably so. Because a critic, especially an uncompromising, merciless one who crosses the line is taking a gamble. Risking his head, in fact. Vultures and other predators wait to trip him up. And smack their lips as they wait. The former victims chomp at the bit and plot their revenge.

Now the die is cast, the leap has been taken. The critic from now on is open to criticism and too bad for him if he gets massacred. He's ready to take the risk.

He had long dreamed of an extended stay in Paris, like all those expatriate American writers of the Lost Generation – F. Scott Fitzgerald, the leader, Hemingway, Dos Passos – and later, Henry Miller, in Clichy. The betrayal was the trigger. All things considered, this all came about because of the betrayal. His happiness, his joy. Thanks, Mom. Especially because she is paying his living expenses.

In New York, he never got anywhere. Too close. Distance was necessary. When he explained that to his mother in early May, she understood, which was, after all, the least she could do. Perhaps she also understood that she'd gone too far, that evening, and wanted to be forgiven. Is the fling with Iouri over? He has no idea. She avoids the subject in the messages she sends him regularly – every three days – on the web. Nor does he ask any questions. The hurt – pride, probably, but that is the most painful – is still too fresh. Whether she understood it or not, she was never the type to skimp and gave him a duplicate of her credit card, recommending he not go overboard! Him! How could he stop himself? Going overboard is synonymous with him; he is excessive, passionate, and has always been that way. Going too far is part of his charm. At least he likes to think so.

He looked on the web for a hotel in Saint-Germain-des-Prés – he insisted – and found one that had a weekly rate. Six hundred euros: very reasonable for Paris, breakfast not included. He doesn't give a damn. There is a bistro next door – in Paris, one business out of two is a food establishment – where he can have his café au lait and his croissant as soon as he gets out of bed.

The name appealed to him from the start: Hôtel du Bout du monde – the end of the world. I'll write at the end of the world, in the middle of nowhere. But it's not in the middle of nowhere, it's on Rue de Seine, just steps from mythical Boulevard Saint-Germain. The Luxembourg Gardens are not far, nor are the second-hand book-sellers. Andy likes to stroll along the banks of the Seine, leaf through books, then sit down for a moment in front of Notre Dame with his finds, and watch tourists craning their necks, photographing the gargoyles with their cell phones. He doesn't take photos. Everything is in his head. He picked up a map of the city, two or three guides – *Promenades littéraires*, the *Manuel de Saint-Germain-des-Prés* by Boris Vian, of which he doesn't understand much, and biographies: of Jean Cocteau, Sartre, and Prévert. He's rereading *A Moveable Feast*, in which Hemingway describes his jaunts through the City of Light.

He made Mimi – Lili in his play; she will recognize herself and not be flattered – a singer who's seen better days, thin, dressed in black, wearing too much makeup. Hermann, her son, is having a passionate affair with Alex Délire – that's the name he finally gave him – a short-lived, vaguely revolutionary poet, hovering around the leaders of the surrealist movement. Hovering and fluttering. For if love is blind, he, Andy, is not. No question of making a phoenix out of a sparrow. Or a robin, to be generous. People who flatter their models are fake artists. The genuine ones paint them as they are, even overdo it sometimes; they have every right. So Alex flutters, Hermann – he made him the publisher of a specialized literary journal with a limited readership – is dying of love, while the spider, Lili, spins her web in the wings.

That's where he's at. Run out of gas. The essential conclusion is not coming. Isn't it always the end that causes the problem? It's the same in human relationships. In the beginning, there is hope, amazement, wonder. Enthusiasm. The end drags on endlessly. Should he kill off Lili? Or Alex? Will Hermann kill one or the other? And what would the murder weapon be? He pictured a half-dozen of them – like in the game Clue that he loved as a child and never tired of playing with his mother – without deciding on one in particular. He doesn't see himself brandishing a candlestick, even in solid gold, and the dagger and the revolver lack originality. As for a rope – too vulgar, really. He could also kill himself, which would be in keeping with logic, but Andy cannot resign himself to knock off his alter ego.

He has set himself a strict schedule to which he adheres. Myriam gave him three months, not a day more. He therefore arises at seven thirty every morning – he sets his alarm clock in the evening before going to bed. A shower, a quick visit to the café downstairs for his croissants and café au lait, while rereading what he wrote the day before. Many writers do that, he knows. A most beneficial exercise: After a night of refreshing sleep, errors – repetitions, anachronisms and redundancy – not seen the day before hit us in the face.

Then he returns to his room and works until one p.m. Works, that is to say he ponders, corrects and crosses out. His first draft is written by hand, with the Montblanc. Then he goes out for lunch. He uses that time to take notes. He is certainly not the first to write in bistros. He always brings his notebook – a Clairefontaine bought here (squared paper, Mediterranean blue cover), and his pen, just in case. You never know when the muse will decide to appear. For the muse is a whimsical entity. It appears and disappears at whim and too bad for us if we don't catch it when it's there. It can take days before it condescends to return.

People speak of Melpomene, of course, Muse of tragedy, though sometimes he also summons Thalia to lighten the atmosphere a bit – not as often, as he is not writing light comedy, a genre he abhors, even French. The meal completed, he returns and works until eight p.m. – transcribing onto the computer this time – then goes out to dinner. One evening a week, he goes out to a play or a concert. On those evenings, he dines after the show, frugally. He has gone to two museums and seen three movies. Two museums is not much, of course, but he exercises restraint. He hasn't come here as a tourist. He goes to bed at one o'clock, reads a bit that falls asleep, exhausted. More sensible than he cannot be imagined – especially in a city such as Paris.

For his outings, he prefers the legendary bars and cafés that all those artists haunted in the last century: Le Dôme, La Rotonde, Le Café de la Paix – where one night Hemingway didn't have enough to pay the bill – La Closerie des Lilas – Trotsky played chess there with Lenin or Apollinaire – the Ritz bar – Hemingway ordered seventy-three martinis for himself and the soldiers who were with him – Harry's New York Bar, Brasserie Lipp – Hemingway feasted on the potatoes in oil and the *cervelas*, as Andy read in his book – Le Falstaff where Fitzgerald, completely drunk, refereed a boxing match between Hemingway, him again, and Morley Callaghan. The latter got the first knockout, which seems to have sounded the death knell on their friendship. And Le Flore, of course, and Les Deux Magots. An embarrassment of riches.

All these places enchant him. And inspire him.

Today he's heading to Harry's Bar. He wants a club sandwich – a touch of nostalgia, as he experiences from time to time for the gastronomy, as it were, of the Big Apple. For let's be honest: The sandwich in question has nothing gastronomical about it. It is, however, comforting. At eighteen and a half euros, it is not cheap of course,

125

but in Paris, everything is expensive. In New York too. Besides, there like here, it's the setting that counts. That of Harry's Bar is worth its weight in euros. James Bond himself went there when his missions brought him to Paris.

Perhaps he will begin with a Bloody Mary. Legend has it was invented at Harry's Bar, in the twenties, by a bartender named Petiot – wasn't that also the name of a famous murderer who killed sixty or so Jews during the Second World War? He also read somewhere, in one of his guides or else on the web, that some people in France called the cocktail *menstruation de Mary* – Mary's menstruation. A flagrant lack of taste, if it is indeed true. Another urban legend no doubt; he doesn't really believe it. He himself has never heard it. In any case, not at Harry's Bar – he would never have drunk it.

He has no date, but he almost always meets interesting people there. A Canadian the other time – John Paradis, a name no one could invent– a Francophone Quebecer who spoke English without a trace of an accent. A retired professor of literature, a lover of Proust like himself. He was immersed in *Le temps retrouvé* when Andy noticed the cover of the book, which explains why he approached him. A very cultured guy. He knew details about the life of the great man that Andy himself didn't. The famous *Bible of Amiens* by Ruskin, for example, that Proust translated – five years of labour, they say – before tackling his *À La Recherche du temps perdu*, well, it was his mother who did the first translation. She translated during the day; he corrected at night. But when Proust submitted the manuscript to the publisher in 1901, the name of Jeanne didn't even appear on the list of contributors. "A selfless woman," John Paradis said, philosophically.

"A true mother," Andy replied, more vehemently than he would have liked.

The other looked at him, a bit surprised.

"You think so?"

Andy shrugged his shoulders. He wasn't going to tell his troubles to a stranger.

"That must be what they call a ghostwriter," John Paradis said.

Andy corrected him: "In this case, a ghost translator. We mustn't confuse the creator with his interpreter."

"Translators are often ghosts, alas. And yet, what would readers do without them?"

"They would make the effort to learn other languages. Like you and I."

"I only speak two," John Paradis said. "But I've read authors who write in a good hundred languages that I wouldn't have the time to learn. And if I took the time to learn them, I'd no longer have time to read the authors. Let's not shoot the messenger."

Andy had to admit that he was right.

A most instructive conversation over a glass or two – three, in fact – of bourbon.

Then, last week, that incredibly handsome actor. Lukas – "my friends call me Luke" – Balta, who portrays a supercop in the popular TV series broadcast all over the planet, in France as well. On Canal Plus. Andy watched an episode last night in bed. Hilarious to hear it in French. You sometimes wonder what their criteria are in choosing the voices. Dante Sullivan – that's the name of the cop in question – they call Dant', as if the *é* that is so musical in Italian and in English were an insignificant silent *e*. As for Sullivan, Andy will never be able to pronounce it like them. No matter how much you pucker up your lips, the *u* in French is simply unpronounceable. Even after five weeks of immersion in Paris, he can't do it.

The character is Irish. But how to convey his accent, which Andy finds charming? In yesterday's episode, Dante Sullivan expressed himself like any Parisian – using slang. And they ask people to take him seriously! Andy laughed throughout almost the entire show, and the storyline had nothing funny about it. A psychopath – another one – drawing his inspiration from *lingchi*, a Chinese form of torture, to cut his victims, children that he kidnapped, into pieces with an Exacto knife. And Luke assured him that all episodes are based on genuine crimes committed all over the United States over the last twenty years. It sends chills down your spine.

Before, people followed the investigations of Lieutenant Columbo and the murderers were often likeable; at least you could understand their motivation: greed, jealousy, vengeance. Even shame sometimes: the fear of having some hideous secret from the past exposed.

Circumstances described as attenuating, whether they were or not. Now criminals are just broken-down machines and as for the motive, you can no longer understand a thing.

So many nuances are lost, Andy thinks. Not only humour and poetry. Whatever John Paradis thinks, translation is a stopgap, at best a consolation prize. That's why he categorically refuses to read Proust in English. When he finishes his play, he will take up Russian. For a long time, he has planned to read Dostoevsky in the original Cyrillic.

Dante Sullivan, the Jaguar. Strangely, in French they say "cou-guar." In English that would have been inconceivable. *Cougar* desig-nates an aging – and more or less well-off – woman who treats herself to young gigolos. Like Mimi. In French too, according to what he's been told. Except that they omit the second U, and write it like the English … But well, they still called him "couguar"; who knows why. Lukas – Luke – had a good laugh when he told him that. He doesn't take himself seriously. Not yet. A point in his favour.

In any case, they exchanged email addresses and who knows, as they say. Not that he has a chance – not a shadow of one. The handsome feline is quite obviously hetero. Unwavering. An area in which Andy is never wrong. Especially as he seemed partial, to say the least, to Marjorie Dubois, a young Canadian actress who played a small part – scarcely more than an extra – in his series. But it was also she who played the duchess in the fateful play, the one Andy had panned in his review. Fortunately, Lukas had seemed unaware of that. Perhaps their exchange would have been less cor-dial had he known.

He imagines him in the role of Alex. He did have a quick word with him about it and Luke seemed interested. They both agreed on one fact: An actor must play a wide range of characters. Now Luke Balta is too closely identified with Dante Sullivan. It's bad for his im-age. He doesn't want to play righters of wrongs his whole life. So yes, why not a hypersensitive poet, disenchanted, a bit of a loser? He'll talk to his agent about it.

For his own character, Hermann, Andy is not yet sure. He can't manage to give him another face than his own. As for Lili … It's no good; it's his mother whom he sees.

Oddly, and fortunately, in fact, his resentment wanes as the writing of his play progresses. Of course art, writing in particular, is a catharsis. Specialists of all types have repeated it in every possible way a thousand times. Music brings another kind of deliverance. So does painting. But writing ... Mimi will probably be forgiven when he finishes his play. Mother and son will rediscover the deep bond they share. Knowing that removes a thorn from his side.

He walks, not hurrying, but strolling. The city enchants him, as we've already said. Is Paris not a celebration? Especially as the weather today ... Just splendid. A glorious day. That's the word that's been in his head since this morning. Glorious. A glorious, can you say *une journée glorieuse* in French? Fabulous weather, a magnificent day. A day of glory. Everything smiles upon him. Perhaps he'll meet someone, someone unexpected, will be thunderstruck by someone. He'll find out how to end his play.

He walked through the Jardin des Tuileries and is now on Rue de Rivoli. A little farther, on Boulevard des Capucines, is the Café de la Paix and its Napoléon mille feuille. The best mille feuille in the world according to his gastronomic guide. And it's true; Andy has checked. He is tempted to return there. They have that brandade – cod and artichoke hearts – that made him swoon the last time. Especially as Proust mentioned the café – Saint-Loup dined there one evening with Rachel, his mistress ... No, it will be Harry's Bar, as planned.

Because mille feuille and brandade, really ... Too difficult to work after such a feast. He eats too much – and too much fat, too much rich food, unquestionably. He must have gained twenty-five pounds since he's been here. Or rather ten kilos – it always sounds less dire in metric. It's just that in Paris there are so many restaurants and everywhere is good. Except for the tourist traps in the Latin Quarter. He doesn't go to them.

But ten kilos, that's a fact. The excess weight is a serious handicap when it comes to his powers of seduction, as he himself realizes. His figure was not lanky to begin with. And in his case, it is certainly not muscle mass. Even though he wears loose-fitting shirts, he can't manage to camouflage his love handles. Yet he walks every day, in the traces of Ernest Hemingway, F. Scott Fitzgerald and Zelda, Gertrude Stein and Ezra Pound. His predecessors, he likes to think. Because he too will have his name in a guide one day. *Andy N. Bloch was at Harry's New York Bar, that is where he wrote the last act of* ... he'll be glad when he finds the title ... *the last act of his masterpiece. Why not?*

But following in the traces of those people, all gourmets, if you believe the gossip, and almost all alcoholic – it's true they were fleeing Prohibition – you always end up in a bistro. And once there, how to resist? You order a ham sandwich on baguette to go with your glass of beer, then a second glass of beer to finish the ham sandwich. He scarcely dares imagine Mimi's face if she knew she were paying for such un-kosher snacks. But in France, you do as the French, especially as he has a weakness for ham. Even in New York he sometimes succumbed to his vice. The prosciutto he bought in Little Italy and then ate alone at home, a bit ashamed, but satisfied ... After dessert, a good-quality brandy – a fine Grande Champagne when you can treat yourself – to get the coffee up on its feet.

And their bread, how to resist? When they put the basket on the table, he doesn't resist. He even asks for more when they bring him the main course.

What to say about the sauces, the cakes and the cheeses? Croissants at breakfast? One should be enough with his café au lait, yet he has two – sometimes a chocolate one – when he should stick to melba toast – no butter – and lemon tea.

But the butter, the butter from Normandy, or, even better, the butter from Brittany, salted ...

And the wine ...

There are countless temptations, alas. An epicurean such as himself succumbs; he cannot do otherwise.

Now he is on Rue de la Paix. Deep in rumination, distracted, he suddenly collides with ... a vision. A vision in black – T-shirt, jeans, sneakers. A two or three-day-old beard, also black, darkens his hollow cheeks. Andy has time to see his eyes: impenetrably dark like the water of a lake at night. Narrow hips, flat stomach: He sees that too, in a flash. Slim, without being scrawny, however. A gold chain around his neck. But Andy can't make out what's at the end of the chain.

"Sorry," he stammers, stupidly.

Stupidly because perhaps it was the other one who bumped into him. He always tends to feel guilty. The Judeo-Christian feeling par excellence, guilt. Simply Judeo in his case, but that's more than enough. Born that way. You cannot free yourself of it; it poisons your entire life.

And stupidly because if he'd found something witty to say, and usually he is known for his subtle witticisms, they could have engaged in conversation.

The other one disappeared as abruptly as he appeared in his life. Dematerialized, as it were.

Andy remains frozen for a moment. Perhaps this was the un-hoped-for encounter for which he had hoped. He was unable to seize the opportunity.

To begin with, where had he come from? Fallen from heaven?

The fallen angel. Lucifer, the handsomest of angels, the most brilliant. But also the most vain – and he was absolutely right to be so. The rebel. Fallen from heaven, yes. Thrown into Gehenna – on that score, perhaps Andy is confused. It doesn't matter – he has just found his title: *Sleepless Nights in Gehenna*. And it doesn't matter either that the angel flew away. He found the ending. The collision with the angel – Lucifer, the bearer of light – has illuminated him.

Sleepless Nights … An almost Dostoevskian title. Dostoevsky too spoke of nights when tormented souls sought sleep in vain. His Gehenna was St. Petersburg in the summer solstice when the sun basically does not set. *White Nights*. What they call "nuits blanches" in French. And today is the day of the solstice. Everything is connected.

He quickens his step. He'll be glad when he's seated at a table at Harry's Bar. He's afraid of losing his idea. That's already happened to him, and more than once. An idea appears, but you don't have a pen and paper with which to jot it down. And when you finally have them, the idea is no longer there. Or else, and in a way it is even more

131

frustrating, you're in a rush, you jot down a word to remember – a vital clue – and when you see it again a few hours later, you no longer remember the connection: The clue is useless. Whimsical muse.

He repeats his idea to himself, turns it over in his head. It will be like Don Juan in the opera, in the final scene, when the ground suddenly opens beneath the bad guy – though Andy tends to find him rather likeable in his own way – and he is swallowed up.

In his own play, it will be Lili.

Such a thing would never happen in real life – life is too predictable, alas, or fortunately – but we are in the theatre. And in the theatre, everything is allowed.

There. He has his revenge. And if she isn't flattered, Mimi will be proud of him.

He enters Rue Daunou almost at a run. Harry's Bar, finally, at number five – *Sank Roo Doe Noo*, as the sign in the window amusingly indicates. He enters. Twenty people maximum, but no familiar faces; so much the better. He won't waste time greeting people and exchanging trivialities. He chooses a table, orders his sandwich: chicken, egg, tomato, lettuce, no ham, please – today, he's decided to be sensible; he's already departed from the rules too much since he's been in Paris – a glass of draft beer. He prefers to abandon the idea of a Bloody Mary; he wants to keep his mind very clear. He takes out his pen and notebook. Then he calls back the waiter: "No chips either, please," he says – because here, they serve club sandwiches with chips rather than with French fries, like in the United States. But chips also make you put on weight and Andy is determined to not indulge in any more excess. "And an Evian instead of the glass of beer."

The end is near; he can finally catch sight of land. Tonight, perhaps. Or in two or three days. He will devote the final month to putting the finishing touches on his work. In Biarritz or, better yet, in Normandy, in Trouville – at the luxurious Hôtel Roches Noires where Proust stayed with his mother, in summer. He's heard that you can request to see his room. You can even stay in it if it's vacant. A possibility that makes Andy euphoric. He'll treat himself to this reward, regardless of the price – sure to be astronomical. He certainly deserves it.

For me, passion was all that mattered, he jots down in his notebook. It's Hermann speaking, of course. The line was right; he just had the wrong character, earlier. She replies …

What Lili would have replied we will never know. When the homemade bomb explodes, that's where he's at. It is he who falls into the abyss.

10

On the Terrace of the Majestic, in Mexico City

People think of the night that
they called, that they still call
La Noche Triste.

... he did not spare the young
actress who, very half-heartedly
in his opinion, portrayed the duchess.

She is returning from Tacuba, northwest of Mexico City. She was determined to see that tree, the *ahuehuete*, at the foot of which Hernando Cortés had cried at the end of La Noche Triste, the Night of Sorrows, June 30, 1520, when the Spanish, surrounded, tried to flee Tenochtitlán despite the bridges being cut off. She found it strange that people remember it, remember that Cortés cried. It was perhaps the first, the only time in his life. Or else he cried when he was alone, never in front of his men. But he'd lost half his army.

The name of the tree, a Mexican cypress, comes from a Nahuatl word, *ahuehuetl*, and means "old water tree" because it grows on the shores of lakes and rivers, its roots submerged for part of the year. It still has leaves; new ones grow before the old ones are ready to fall. A venerable tree, known for its longevity. In Oaxaca, there's one that's two thousand years old.

She came to Mexico to gather information, to immerse herself too, breathe the air of the country. Her name is Marjorie Dubois – from her real name Marjolaine Brisebois – and she's slated to play the female lead in the next film by Ivan Cristu, the rising star in the firmament of directors. He has two films to his credit. The first, which lasts twenty-two minutes and seven seconds (he's attached to the seven seconds, the final still frame of beauty, or cruelty, which was described as almost unbearable), created a sensation, unusual for a short film.

The second, a feature film this time, caused a real commotion: seven nominations and two Oscars, best editing – he edits his own films – best original screenplay – he writes his own screenplays – last year. Plus an array of awards and distinctions at various film festivals where his work has been presented. He chose Marjorie to portray Malintzin in his upcoming film, *Noche Triste*. Malintzin, or Doña Marina, Mallinali Tenépal, La Malinche, the Aztec interpreter of Hernando Cortés, his companion and the mother of his son Martín, the first official Mestizo in Mexico. Or simply *la lengua*, language, in the missives that the conquistador addressed to the king.

She still doesn't believe it. Ever since she did the ad for Nutella two years ago, fortune has continued to smile on her. "I can't resist. Give me more," she whispered, lips smeared with chocolate spread. She also dubbed it in French – *je ne résiste pas, encore, encore* – she speaks both languages fluently, with just a trace of an accent, a distinctive way of pronouncing her Rs, in both languages.

So chocolate was the springboard to fame. First, she landed the role of Lola in *Lola la nuit*, the remake of *Broken Wings*, a classic from the late forties. Filming will begin next August in Vancouver and the film is scheduled for release in spring the following year if all goes well. A low-budget art film, but the industry has great hopes for it. Then, a tiny role as a junkie in a detective series, a brief appearance, so to speak, three lines – she went unnoticed. However, in March, one thing leading to another, and against all expectations, she was given the part of Georgiana, on a Broadway stage, no less, in *Moriarty and the Duchess of Devonshire* by Juliette Evanelli.

Thirteen performances only, an unlucky number. The play was not a success, despite its author being incredibly well-known. Yet her performance was greeted by a chorus of praise – with the exception of the article in *Big Apple Scene*, a venomous article penned by one Andy N. Bloch, filled with sarcasm about her. Not only about her, in fact. The entire play – author, director, cast, set designer – was put to the sword. Regarding her, he wrote – she knows the passage by heart: *They say that just one of the Duchess of Devonshire's smouldering looks would light the cigars or pipes of the men who crowded around her. Tonight, the poor woman's bones must have been knocking together in their grave before the insipid young actress who portrayed her. While Miss Dubois – and this isn't the unforgettable Blanche, far from it – has pretty eyes, since I'm not one to withhold credit where credit is due, her qualities end there. And as pretty as they are, they're far from being enough to make her an actress worthy of that name. I point out, however, not that this excuses her, that actors worthy of that name are conspicuous by their absence.* He went on to pan her two partners, John Wallace (Sherlock Holmes) and Brian Fuller (Moriarty). Only the ostrich father that adorned the duchess' fuchsia hat found grace in the eyes of that wet blanket. *A success!*

And that review appeared in the most prestigious – although it has only three thousand subscribers – magazine in the New York theatre world. Other magazines fortunately had another point of view. But to be honest: Whatever Marjorie thinks or would like to think, it was not exactly a chorus of praise. They did, however, laud her sensitive, subtle acting, and spoke of her elegance combining freshness and maturity and of her accent described as indefinable and exquisite. Pages were devoted to her in various widely read magazines. But she mostly remembers the murderous article, the one impossible to erase from her mind. The word insipid above all seemed to be inscribed in indelible ink.

Not that her role was very demanding, not like that of Lola or of Malintzin. The plot was based on an authentic event, the theft of a Gainsborough painting: the portrait of the Duchess of Devonshire by a swindler – Moriarty in the play. Portraying the duchess consisted mainly of strutting about on stage, wearing the famous hat, waving her fan, and seducing, even at times humiliating, her abductor. Because she emerged from the painting at night, simpering in Professor Moriarty's fantasies. Deep down, it was not she who was insipid, but the mediocre lines she had to deliver.

However, she was acting on Broadway, and that counts. Delivering lines and strutting about still had to be done with grace, as has been observed. At one point, she cried. Real tears. Moriarty was keeping her prisoner; she begged him to set her free. She wanted to return to her painting. It hadn't been difficult to cry. She only had to think of that review. It had been a slap in the face, and her cheek was still burning. And all you had to do was listen to the coughing and throat clearing in the theatre. Quite obviously, the audience was bored: another reason to cry.

And yet it was this scene that had convinced Ivan Cristu, who came me to see the play on the last night. On a whim, tired of palm trees, as he told Marjorie, he'd decided to spend a few days in New York, filling his lungs with polluted air. There, a capricious friend – "she changes her mind like she changes dresses, and she has a lot" – had given him her ticket. Sometimes fate turns out to be a blessing. A few days later, the impulsive Cristu offered her the role. She auditioned for the sake of form: She'd already been selected. Even if, in the film, it is not she who cries.

She doesn't have the physique of a Native, quite the contrary. Chestnut hair, grey-green eyes – but he said he was not looking for a physique, he was looking for a soul. "You have that soul." The colour of her eyes was incidental, he added. The least of his worries. Plausibility is not overburdened by such trivial details. She agrees with him: In the time of Victor Hugo, of Dumas (father and son), ageing actresses, sometimes even obese, often played ingénues in the theatre. And audiences believed them. Sarah Bernhardt played *La Dame aux Camélias* at age fifty; she was close to sixty when she portrayed a teenager in *L'Aiglon*.

Marjorie also has an accent, another point in her favour. A French accent, but who knows what a Nahuatl accent was like back then? The Nahuatl accent of a girl who chose to express herself in Spanish; no one has any idea. The film will be shot in English. And Marjorie will speak with her very slight French accent.

She's back from Tacuba. Before returning to her hotel, the Majestic, she walked around Mexico City's historic centre. Eyes wide open behind her sunglasses, she entered the old temple and the impressive cathedral. She walked along a street called Isabel la Católica. The entire past with its rivers of silver and gold, its rivers of blood. Processions of feathered priests, their embroidered tunics, flowers strewn along Montezuma's way. Then the Spanish in armour, on their prancing horses.

In a few split seconds, she saw all that. Overcome, swallowed up by history. Feeling as if she were moving in a dream. She only had to close her eyes. Not even. Even with eyes open, you can dream. Someone, she can't remember who, once said that dreams are our only true reality. Why not? Deep down, she likes that idea. And dreams are like the movies. Someone, and she knows perfectly who, already told her that she was his fantasy since the Nutella ad appeared on TV.

Then it began to rain, a violent rain that, with no warning, beat down upon the city. She thought of *La Noche Triste*, when torrential rain poured over Tenochtitlan, when the solders disappeared into the lagoon, burdened by the weight of stolen gold, unable to swim. Died rich, as they'd dreamed of being one day, one commentator wrote, not without irony. Death is the ultimate justice. A routed army, and blood everywhere, cries of distress and pain, cries of terror. Buried treasure. Death, a black figure, with its scythe. Noxious odours hung in the air. Hocks severed, flanks pierced, the horses died miserably on the shores. Yes, the proud horses that had filled the Indians with marvel bled to death with pitiful convulsions. Marjorie saw the frantic retreat, could hear the horses whinnying, the cries. The survivors advanced in the mud, amid the excrement, stepped over the dying and the corpses. Cortés cried at the foot of a cypress.

She ran back, took a hot bath in the lion claw bathtub, then went up to the Terraza. On the hotel roof, as a matter of fact. With a view of the Zócalo, the Templo Mayor, the cathedral, all the imposing past, the city's bloody past at her feet. She ordered a margarita. Now the sky is cloudless. It is seven thirty in the evening. Julio Martín Rebolledo has just arrived, limping slightly.

He, as usual, was caught in a traffic jam – Mexicans, at least those who live in the Federal District, always are. Otherwise there are demonstrations for this, against that, that block their access. When they make an appointment, they set a time and it can be any time, but always after the time set. Or else they say *ahorita* and it's the same thing. Any time. They have another concept of time.

But today, Julio is only half an hour late.

Ivan Cristu hired him as a consultant on the film: He has a doctorate in history and is a specialist of the Conquest and of Aztec culture. He also teaches Nahuatl at the Autonomous University. For the next two weeks, he must teach Marjorie Dubois a basic knowledge of the language. Have her repeat in a credible way the few words she may – the dialogue is not yet finalized – have to say in the Aztec language.

This evening, they're meeting up to get to know one another. The classes as such will begin tomorrow at the same time – that is, approximately. They will take place in Marjorie's room, in her suite, actually. In the daytime, Marjorie will go to the sites reminiscent of the episode of the Conquest. *Immerse yourself,* Ivan Cristu had advised her.

He stares at her, baffled. Dressed unpretentiously: black jeans, white T-shirt, black sneakers on her feet. No jewellery except for a ring on her right index finger. A cat's eye. A watch on her left wrist. Chestnut hair tied on the nape of her neck with a ribbon, also black, grey eyes. Or green? Really, they couldn't have found anyone less true to life to portray a Native princess. Okay, she's pretty, but pretty isn't enough. Malinche was far more than that. It is as if Andy N. Bloch, whose reviews he's never read, is prompting him. *Having pretty eyes is not enough.*

He suppresses a gesture of impatience. Really, this is nonsense. These gringos think that anything goes. They take hold of history, theirs or someone else's, and distort it to reflect them.

Although gringo ... In the case of Ivan Cristu, it isn't so obvious. The word usually designates an American, and Cristu really isn't one. According to what we know, at least. Because in terms of his private life, he is unyielding and says nothing. He was born in the Balkans, in Dobruja, a territory on the shores of the Black Sea shared by the Romanians and the Bulgarians. He is thirty-eight years old: That's about all he's revealed about himself.

Apparently he lives as a hermit somewhere in California. But where? Certainly not in Bel Air, Beverly Hills, Santa Monica or in other glitzy places of the movie world. In Northern California, probably, or perhaps at the Mexican border. He drives an antique, an enormous Daimler from the fifties, midnight blue. An eccentric. "My movies speak for me," he declared in one of the rare interviews he deigned to give. "My story belongs only to me." He is indeed right. "The person who will write my biography has not yet been born." He is rarely seen. He wasn't even at the Academy Awards last year. The producer accepted the statuettes on his behalf. Cannes, Venice, Toronto, Berlin: Everywhere he was conspicuous by his absence.

It is also known that his masters are Orson Welles, "for his amazing compositions," Luis Buñuel, for his "surreal humour," and Robert Elkis, "for his interplay of light and shadow." But as opposed to Elkis, he writes his screenplays, as we've said. Elkis derived his inspiration from novels – very often detective novels and very often mediocre ones – that he improved.

"Nothing original, as you can see," he muttered in his beard before returning to his lair. Obviously won over, the journalist concluded that he was too modest: If we rely on his first feature film, Ivan Cristu, "the Balkan Bear," as she nicknamed him – the nickname has clung to him ever since – is without question the most original director of his generation.

"I don't have the physique for the job," Marjorie says. She must have read his thoughts, understood that she hasn't passed the test. Or has done so with difficulty.

"I of course imagined a different Malinche," Julio replies cautiously.

A Mexican one, he continues in his mind. Malinche belongs to the Mexicans. Indian. With dark eyes, black hair, high cheekbones, and a bronzed complexion. You're nothing like that. You have the part because you're sleeping with Cristu.

"But I will have black hair, of course. I'm used to changing colour. Actors are chameleons. Last month, I had auburn hair, almost red. An ad for perfume. I went back to my natural colour to play Lola. My next film."

In the original, Lola was blond, but Nicholas, the director, prefers her the way she is. Chestnut hair.

"As for my grey eyes … Ivan Cristu said that eye colour didn't count; he was looking for the soul. Anyway, the film will be shot in black and white."

As were the two previous films. Inspired by Bob Elkis, Cristu swears only by shadows and light. The great tradition, he says. But a tradition that he reinvents. He uses colour extremely sparingly: It pops up – dazzles, disorients, astounds – when you least expect it. The seven last seconds of the short film. He also superimposes languages. Without subtitling – and people understand.

She casts a glance around. "Julio … should I call you Julio or Señor Martín?"

"Julio."

"Is smoking allowed here, Julio? In Canada, no point in asking, it's not."

"Not here either."

"Tobacco originated in America; you're abandoning your traditions. I've heard people say that traditions must be shaken up. Ivan Cristu thinks so too. I don't know … Did people smoke in the time of the Aztecs? … No, people drank chocolate. For me, everything began with chocolate. A promotional clip for Nutella."

The girl makes him feel dizzy. She's agitated. Overexcited. He pictures Malinche as calm, almost serene when faced with her destiny.

"You can't smoke, but you can drink tequila."

He motions to the waiter.

"They smoked and drank hot chocolate, but only on certain occasions. It wasn't the everyday pleasure it's become."

The waiter approaches their table. Julio orders two tequilas *con sangrita* – a spicy mixture of tomato, orange and lime juice with jalapeno peppers – *antojitos con salsas*. Margaritas are for tourists, he says to Marjorie, pushing aside her glass. *Los gringos.*

Their conversation goes back and forth between French and Spanish – which Marjorie mangles. She suggested that they use the familiar *tu*; she becomes confused with *usted*. Not only with *usted*, Julio thinks.

"It's strange," he says – in French – "these Canadians seeking La Malinche's soul. Last winter I met another one who was also looking for it. Mathilde."

"Did she find it?"

He smiles – an indecipherable smile, a bit disillusioned. "She's writing a thesis on the issue of betrayal in translation. An issue as old as translation itself."

He thinks back to that unsuccessful evening.

Mathilde had come to the conference he'd organized in mid-December at the university. She attended his presentation and approached him at the end. Hungry for information about La Malinche, with a thousand questions about the treacherous or liberating role that she and translation had played in the conquest of Mexico. Completely obsessed. For the three days of the conference, there had been explicit looks between them, light touches that seemed involuntary, but that were not. In short, they both knew without saying what they expected from one another. The next-to-last evening – she'd remained two weeks in all – she'd invited him to her place, to the house that Professor Vásquez had loaned her in Coyoacán. Supposedly to talk to him about her research, to ask him advice. She'd made margaritas.

Just as he was leaving the university, he found himself stuck between two friends he couldn't shake off who insisted on going with him, who knows why. With the help of tequila, the discussion grew acrimonious. Balta (one of the two) at times behaves abominably when he has had too much to drink. Mathilde seemed disappointed, irritated. As for him, well, he alas felt less and less spirited as the evening progressed.

Then his cell phone rang. It was his wife, panic-stricken. Their daughter Xannath – they had given her an Aztec name – age three, had been vomiting all evening. She had to be driven to the hospital: It was urgent. He dashed out and his friends followed him.

In the end, she simply had gastroenteritis as children often do. He didn't see Mathilde again. He'd sent her an email a week later to wish her happy new year. She'd responded icily. *Feliz año nuevo y muchos exitos en tus proyectos.*

"Did she find it?" Marjorie says again.

He gives a start. "Pardon?"

"That Canadian. Did she find La Malinche's soul?"

"I don't think so."

The waiter returns with their drinks, a basket of corn chips and two salsas in their small dishes, one spicy and the other less so.

"Gracias," Marjorie says.

In Spanish, you have to roll your R's and it isn't easy. She read that "Nahuatl" means "that pleases the ear." And also "language of the gods." The R sound does not exist in Nahuatl. The Aztecs called Cortés Malinche, which really is ironic. Giving a macho guy like him a woman's name – even if it was his companion. But it also reveals her importance in the eyes of the Indians.

"A kind of Bloody Mary," she observes.

"Mexican."

She said that because of the alcohol and tomato juice association. Here each is served in its own small glass and you drink from them alternately.

He smiles. A sincere smile, this time. Finally.

"So she was a translator?" she asks. "The one who was seeking Malinche's soul."

"If you like. More of a translation studies scholar. She's interested in the history of translation."

"Yes, in fact, in terms of translation, I was wondering … Apparently Emperor Cuauhtémoc, when Cortés tortured him, said he was not lying on a bed of roses. Were there roses in Mexico? Or was that a translation of La Malinche's? Because … I don't know … I was under the impression that the cultivation of roses was European or even Chinese. But American? And I find it strange that he said that while the soles of his feet were being burned."

Mathilde had asked almost the same question on that last evening. She'd also wondered about the love that perhaps existed between Cortés and La Malinche. On that topic, people could wonder until the end of time. The Conqueror of course never spoke of it in his letters. As for Malintzin's feelings, who knows them?

"It was not Cortés who tortured him," Julio says patiently. "It was the treasurer, Julián de Alderete. Cortés is the one who put a stop to the torture."

"I must have read wrong," she says.

She seems mortified.

"Many people make that mistake. People like blaming him with all the sins committed here. Oh, he committed more than his share ..."

"But not that one."

"He was the one, after all, who had him hanged a bit later ... As for the famous phrase, several versions exist. Cuauhtémoc perhaps said: *'¿Estoy yo en un deleite o bano?'* That is: Am I in pleasure or in a bath? Or in a bath of pleasure. Or in a bath for pleasure. All depends on the authors. On the translators. In a tragedy published in Spain in the nineteenth century he was attributed as saying: *'¡Acaso estoy yo sobre rosas!'* And me, am I lying on a bed of roses? Others have spoken of *lecho* or of *cama de rosas,* une couche, a layer, a bed."

"And your personal opinion?"

"My opinion is that historic truth doesn't exist. In the same way that no truth exists with a capital T. The same applies to love. There is no love, there are only proofs of love. That comes from a French poet, Jean Cocteau, if I am not mistaken."

"But you are a history professor, aren't you? A history professor who doesn't believe in historic truth?"

"I try to instil philosophical doubt in my students ... In fact, the bed of roses is never anything but an image. It certainly conveys what he said in Nahuatl, no matter what it is. The meaning is that the treatment he was undergoing was anything but pleasant. One must give the translator a degree of latitude."

She thinks so; it's like the colour of a person's eyes, a detail. Plausibility is not overburdened by that. Roses, bath, pleasure, the sense is the same, of course. It was she who was complicating her life unnecessarily.

"I'm going to go out and smoke a cigarette," she says. "You don't smoke?"

"No."

He stands up at the same time as her, but she says no, no, he doesn't need to go with her. "Just a quick one, ten minutes at the most."

While she is away, Julio wonders if he didn't judge her a bit quickly. She doesn't have the physique, it's true, but she has something else. She seems intelligent. Intelligent: Malinche was that, unquestionably.

"I ordered us each another tequila," he says when she returns.

This time, they also have guacamole.

"Wonderful. Tomorrow we'll just drink purified water … For our Nahuatl classes. So our heads won't get dizzy … Speaking of which, I have another question. Was it Hernán or Hernando Cortés?"

"Hernán, Hernando, Fernando: it's all the same name. Bernal Díaz del Castillo, the chronicler, called him Hernando. Other biographers preferred other first names. In the movie, it will be Hernando."

"It sounds more Spanish … Hernán sounds like a Germanic name, don't you think? I've read a few books on the topic. In one novel Malinche calls him Nando."

"Nando!"

This time, he doesn't just smile, he bursts out laughing. "Nando! I can't wait to tell my students. What book was it? I definitely want to read it. Because if they say that Malinche called Cortés Nando, there must be other gems as well."

"I don't remember exactly. A French novel, I think. I got it from the library."

"A Harlequin?"

"Not really, but that type." She blushes. "I took it in good faith. Ever since I knew I was going to play the part, I've read almost everything I could find on the topic. The books that I didn't have time to read, I brought … Something else: Is it true that Cortés was a redhead? Bizarre for a Spaniard."

"Always stereotypes," he says, sighing. "Dark-haired Mediterraneans with dark eyes, blond Germanics with blue eyes."

"And you're already disappointed that I, with my grey eyes, will portray La Malinche."

"Touché!"

He asks her if she's hungry. No, she says. She has already eaten. Already? He is surprised.

A quesadilla earlier, or a taco, she doesn't really know anymore, when she was visiting the historic centre. It was delicious. But tomorrow, she says, if he'd like to introduce her to authentic Mexican cuisine – not that heavy, unsophisticated cuisine ubiquitous in Tex-Mex restaurants – she won't eat before the Nahuatl class. She's ready to try anything, even fried grasshoppers if they find any.

She says that she doesn't know what to think about Cortés. Hero, assassin, visionary? She wants to know how Mexicans see him.

"We're descended from both," he replies. "The conquerors and the conquered. From Cortés and from Malinche. We're all Mestizos. When you think of it, the Spanish who came here were Mestizos as well, after seven hundred years of Moorish occupation. A drop of Arab blood must run in my veins."

"My mother is Irish," she says. "My father is Québécois. And they say that all Québécois have a drop of Native blood in their veins."

"So you are Mestizo."

It's true that her eyes are slightly slanted.

"And Malinche? Do Mexicans like or despise her?"

"Some despise her: She is *La Chingada*, the raped. Or the whore. Others pity her: She is the *La Llorona*, the weeping woman. Others love her: Without her, Mexico as it is wouldn't exist. She's the mother of Mexico."

And you?"

"I love her."

"The mother of Mexico, and Cortés would be the father?"

"You can see it that way."

At one point, he excuses himself.

She watches him move away, slightly limping toward the washroom – a sprained ankle he got last week tumbling down a staircase.

"Cortés limped too," she says.

"The aftermath of a love affair that went wrong. With a married woman. He maimed himself running away from the incensed husband. My handicap is less romantic."

Now she's speaking Spanish.

"Me gusta lo que has dicho. De Jean Cocteau. No hay amor."

Yes, perhaps she speaks Spanish like Malinche did. With mistakes and an accent.

"Solo hay pruebas."

She glances at her watch. She must go to her room: She's expecting an important phone call.

Alex, the singer from the Netchaev Group, is supposed to call her at ten o'clock sharp. Four o'clock in the morning for him – they are touring in Europe – the time when he usually goes to bed. The group will do the music for *Lola la nuit*; that's how they met. Alex says that they're working on it, even during their tour. It won't be the old song; it's been heard too often. But they will take inspiration from it. When she returns, Marjorie and he will go on a week's vacation together somewhere in Spain. Perhaps Mallorca or Ibiza.

Julio shrugs his shoulders imperceptibly. The telephone is dampening the proceedings, just as it did last winter with Mathilde.

"What?" she asks.

"Nothing. I was just thinking that history repeats itself."

"History repeats itself."

"Nothing, I assure you. A frivolous thought that crossed my mind … See you tomorrow, Mathilde. Good night."

"Not Mathilde, Marjorie … Malintzin."

Then he smiles. What were you expecting, imbecile? The time of the Conquest, when Cortés could have all the little madams who crossed his path, has passed. In a way, so much the better.

Once alone, he motions to the waiter to bring him the menu. Tonight, he will treat himself to a *mole*.

11

At Jonathan's, a Little Later that Evening

… his friend Mathilde, a translator like himself […] is due to arrive any minute. It's strange," he continues – in French – these Canadians seeking La Malinche's soul. Last winter I met another one who was also looking for it. Mathilde.

"We almost ate shepherd's pie," Jonathan says.

Because, of course, the scandal that Raoul Potvin caused at the End of the World put an end – a brutal end – to the celebration to which they had been unexpectedly invited. They chose to slip away discreetly after the auto-da-fé. Now they are at Jonathan's place. He lives a few streets from the restaurant.

"I don't really understand what happened," Mathilde says.

"Me neither … a dark tale of betrayal, a pact that was not honoured."

"I swear, I couldn't believe my eyes when that big lout with the glasses flicked his lighter."

"It all happened too quickly," Jonathan says. "In the beginning, I thought he wanted to make a joke. Not really funny, but all have our own sense of humour. Plus, that guy didn't exactly seem subtle …"

"And when the other one, the puny guy… Voltaire? The one who won the lottery …"

"Diderot."

"Yes, Diderot. When he started crying ..."

She shivers despite the warmth.

"Well, it was impressive to see two hundred thousand dollars go up in smoke," Jonathan says. "I'd cry too if someone did that to me."

"Impressive, but above all pathetic. It wasn't only money that went up in smoke ... but also ... I don't know ... friendship, trust. Loyalty."

She falls silent. Both picture the scene unfolding: the flame of the lighter touching the lottery ticket that quickly turned into something that twisted and danced, burning fingers, and that Raoul Potvin threw on the ground, crushing it beneath his big foot.

"We don't know the backstory," Jonathan says. "Maybe they had an agreement."

Mathilde doesn't agree. Yes, they had an agreement, but it wasn't the same ticket. Diderot explained that. The other one acted out of pure jealousy. Out of spitefulness.

"I wonder how it ended."

"Badly, for sure. Would you like something to drink?"

On the way over, they bought six bottles of Corona – not forgetting the lime – and a bottle of Muscadet.

"A beer," Mathilde says.

She follows him into the kitchen. Jonathan uncaps two bottles, pours the liquid while tipping the glasses, and slices a lime.

"It was, I don't know ... the cruelty of the gesture," Mathilde says. "Gratuitous cruelty, like in war. You know when soldiers burn an entire village. Stupid cruelty ... Like a world collapsing."

"A world; you're going too far, Mathilde. I grant you that it's a lot of money."

"Two hundred and three thousand dollars. For a poor taxi driver, that's like a million."

"It's still only money. There are worse things."

He's thinking of Fanny, his missing niece.

"Anyway, it broke my heart," Mathilde says. "Do you think he has any recourse?"

"I'd be surprised."

"But we're witnesses. We were there."

"There's no longer any ticket. Besides, we didn't even see the number. How could we testify? We just heard that it was the winning number. Our testimony wouldn't count for much. There is only Diderot's word."

"I wonder ..."

"Impossible. Can you imagine the people who would try to claim sums of money, talking of stolen, lost or burned tickets? No, Mathilde, no ticket, no dough."

She sighs deeply. The evening has gotten off to a bad start. To think they were both thrilled at the idea of spending it together. They don't often get the chance. They haven't seen each other in months. Both are caught up in their own problems, their own affairs. Mathilde is busy writing her thesis; Jonathan is helping his sister Florence and his nephews – because while Fanny has disappeared the two sons remain. And for them, life must go on. For everyone, in fact. Except for Florence, apparently. For her, life seems to have stopped. She can't seem to get back on her feet. Curled up in a ball, devastated.

It was Mathilde who called him yesterday to suggest meeting up. He'd found her a bit mysterious on the telephone. There was something strange about her voice. He was intrigued. They'd agreed to meet at the End of the World in the late afternoon, then go out to dinner somewhere. At first, they hadn't planned to eat there; Jonathan had other plans. That new Moroccan restaurant in the neighbourhood. Or the Japanese. It would be up to her.

After the scene at the End of the World, they walked by the Moroccan place like zombies, not even reading the menu. The Japanese one wasn't on their way. And by joint agreement, they headed to the convenience store to buy beer and wine. Then they found themselves in front of his place.

He shakes himself off. "Well," he said. "We missed the shepherd's pie, but that's no reason to starve. When can I offer you to compensate? Let's see ..."

He opens the refrigerator door – even though he knows what's inside. The remains of a frozen lasagna in its package, three shrivelled radishes and a lettuce that has seen better days. A half a litre of skimmed milk and two eggs. Not even enough to make an omelette.

The pantry is in no better shape. Aside from a few condiments, olive oil, vinegar, Dijon and Meaux mustard, a can of tuna keeps company with a jar of stuffed olives and that's about it. On the counter, the baguette bought the day before yesterday is now hard as a rock. It could come in handy for knocking out a burglar who ventured into the kitchen.

"Sorry. I didn't have time to go shopping."

It's true that he's been eating at Florence's one night out of two. He makes supper – she scarcely touches the contents of her plate, but without him she wouldn't eat at all – then he helps the boys do their homework, tells them a story before tucking them in. He keeps Florence company until midnight, then goes home to work. On the other evening, his mother takes over. Robert takes care of the children on the weekend. Because they're separated now. Florence says it's temporary. Time, for her and for him, to get some semblance of health back. He's on sick leave as well. As well he might. All these catastrophes that have befallen him since last winter. His adopted daughter's lies on TV certainly didn't help. Jonathan had never liked Daphné, while he had a deep bond with Fanny. He'd always found Daphné underhanded: Now he truly hates her.

A crazy life, there's no other word. He thinks with a shiver of anxiety of the children's vacation that's about to begin and the new book he has to translate. How will he get by? He doesn't know. One day at a time, as they say in AA. Since Fanny has gone missing, he feels as if he is living in a dream – a nightmare. Unable to wake up.

"How about ordering a pizza?" Mathilde says. "Vegetarian. It's nice out; we could eat on your terrace."

"Sold," Jonathan says. "I'll call Da Luciano. I have just enough time to run to the green grocer and buy lettuce for salad. They sell it prewashed in a plastic bag."

***

Now they are in Jonathan's back yard, on the small pressure treated wood deck. The wine is in the ice bucket, the salad in the salad bowl. Mathilde made the vinaigrette. The pizza has just arrived.

At first, their conversation is innocuous. They talk about this and that. She suggests that he plant a few annuals: The yard will be more cheerful. But he has no time for gardening. She offers to help him. Next week, if he likes, they could go together to choose them at the market. Herbs as well. She says that he mustn't let himself go.

When the pizza has been eaten, he asks her if she'd like coffee. "The pantry is empty but I do have coffee. I can make us espresso."

She thinks, then decides no, after an espresso she won't sleep all night. A decaf, perhaps, if he has. He doesn't. In that case, she'd rather stick with the wine. A good third of the bottle remains.

"I found you odd, yesterday, on the telephone," he says.

"Odd?"

"Your voice was strange."

She remains silent for a few moments. Something's up, it's true. It's just that she doesn't know how to bring it up. Yet when she phoned yesterday, it was clear in her mind.

"You know that I went to Mexico City last winter," she says.

"For a conference," he says. "You were there when …"

He breaks off. People, even friends, don't like to talk about it. Not out of a lack of compassion. No. More because they don't know how to act. Like at the funeral home when they have to say "My deepest sympathies." People never know how to act to seem sincere. Even when they are.

"Did I tell you I almost fell in love?" she says.

"You didn't tell me anything."

"We don't see each other often enough."

"That's true. How long has it been?"

"Too long. So, I met him at the conference. A specialist in Aztec culture. Tall, dark and handsome, the way I like. His name was, still is Julio Martín. All week, he looked at me …"

"Lustfully?"

"That's what I thought. So I invited him over, on my next-to-last night. I was staying in a magnificent house I had been loaned. You should have seen it – palatial – in Coyoacán. On Malintzin Street, a big coincidence – that's one of Malinche's names. I'd made every-

152

thing: margaritas, guacamole, salsa. All dolled up for the conquest: my long cotton rainbow-coloured skirt, a cashmere sweater bought that same day; I won't tell you what it cost. Polished toe nails. I neglected nothing, you can be sure. He wouldn't be able to resist me. My new perfume, Belle de nuit, sprayed in strategic places. A gold chain around my ankle. Also bought for the occasion."

"A cashmere sweater and a gold chain. You spent a fortune."

"I was getting ready for a hot night; nothing was too good. But the plans fell through and the evening ended more like a *noche triste* … You know, when Cortés lost the battle? No? It's an historic date … In Mexico, anyway. Where was I?"

"Your night of love had fallen through."

"Yes. To begin with, the dark and handsome Latin showed up with two colleagues. Tell me that didn't augur well."

"It augured very badly," Jonathan says, holding back a smile.

"The first one, a descendant of Don Juan, or some manifestation thereof … But she invited me to the conference in Seattle in September, so I didn't lose everything. Speaking of which, is your sister Florence still coming?"

She too had been invited to the conference on little-known women in history. She'd talk about Renée-Pélagie de Sade, the wife of the divine marquis. But right now, in her condition …

"I don't think so, Mathilde."

"I'm sorry …"

"It doesn't matter. Continue your story."

"So I was telling you there were two colleagues. The second one was a braggart who insulted me continuously throughout the evening. A sessional lecturer on the history of Haiti."

"Haiti?"

"He is Haitian."

"And the dark and handsome Latin?"

"In the end, his phone rang, and he left."

"His wife?"

"Or his mistress, his lover, what do I know."

"He must have sensed the ogre in you. Afraid of being devoured. Classic."

She finishes her glass of wine. The bottle is empty in the bucket. She hasn't yet told him the most difficult part. She twists a lock of her hair – a nervous tic of hers.

"You wouldn't have a cigarette?"

"I quit smoking."

"I did too, but I still miss it, especially after eating. You know, the feeling that the meal is not complete."

Jonathan wonders when she'll stop beating around the bush. "So his phone rang …"

"Yes. I didn't tell you the funniest thing. The colleague, the one who kept on insulting me, hit on me when Julio left. He's the one who wanted me. Can you imagine? I showed him the door. Screw a lout like that? Me? No way."

"Are you sure this wasn't something the two of them cooked up beforehand?"

"I asked myself exactly that."

"So let me guess: You emptied the bottle of tequila and spent the rest of the night crying your eyes out."

"It didn't exactly happen like that … One hour later, the doorbell rang. I'm so ridiculously naive I thought it was Julio, tall, dark and handsome, returning. But no, it was the other lout, who wanted to apologize."

"You're not going to tell me that …"

"Yes."

"But three seconds ago, you said it was out of the question."

"I caved … As if I were taking my revenge. It's idiotic, I know."

"You, a married woman! And to think I thought you were fidelity incarnate."

She shuts her eyes for a moment. "It was my last night in Mexico City," she says, sighing, as if to justify herself.

"The second-to-last."

"The second-to-last. Also the last. Both, I mean."

A grey cat furtively wanders into the yard, halts and changes his mind and flees after a few seconds. "I'd like a glass of water," Mathilde says. "No, it's OK, I'll go get it."

"You don't know everything," she says, returning.

She has bought a carafe and two glasses.

"There's worse to come?"

"We exchanged emails. We've been corresponding for six months."

"Erotic messages."

"No, no, not erotic. Well, a bit. Balthazar. I don't even know his last name. His email address is balta1982. His friends call him Balta. And 1982 must be the year he was born, I imagine."

"And?"

"And he's coming here. Perhaps he's already here. In Montreal."

Silence. Jonathan tries to understand, then: "And you want me to …"

She: "Save my life."

"Only that."

She explains: When Balthazar announced he was coming – he has relatives in Montreal – she of course declared that she was married. But now he wants to meet her husband. To say what to him? A mystery. And Luc – the husband – obviously knows nothing about the affair in Mexico City. Telling him is out of the question; He would have a fit. As it is, relations between them have been strained for some time. Soon they will be married ten years.

"So?" Jonathan asks.

The situation is strained, but Luc trusts her. Should he learn what happened, everything would go up in smoke, like the lottery ticket earlier. It's complicated enough as it is; she doesn't want to confuse the issue. On one hand, she still loves Luc. On the other, Balthazar is almost here. Late evening, he'd said. First he has to go to his aunt's and his cousins', drop off his luggage and have dinner with them. He will phone; he has her number. Her cell, of course, not the home number. But he doesn't know her address. So she thought that …

She stops.

"Spit it out," Jonathan says.

She thought she could invite him here.

"Here?"

"To your place. We could … I don't know … we could say you're my husband."

155

"Good God, Mathilde, why don't you arrange to meet him in a café?"

"Because he could follow me. Under no circumstances must he know my address. And certainly not my husband. I fear the worst. But if we meet here, at our place, so to speak, we'll know what he has to say. Then you can talk to him, make him listen to reason."

"Tell him you refuse to introduce him to your husband, that's all."

"I told him that, what do you think? But he insists. If I refuse, my telephone is liable to ring day and night. Imagine if Luc answers when I'm in the shower. It's impossible that because of a little one-night affair …"

"Two."

"My whole life will be ruined."

Light comedy, and at its worst. *Heavens, my husband!*

"How old are you, Mathilde? Listening to you, you sound as if you're going through a teenage crisis."

"You know very well how old I am."

Both telephones – Mathilde's cell and Jonathan's cordless – ring at the same time. Jonathan looks at the call display. It's Florence. He goes into the house to speak to her. Mathilde remains on the deck.

"It was him," she says when he returns.

"Florence," he says. "I have to go. She can't stop crying."

Mathilde nods her head, and Jonathan does too. The evening is ending as badly as it began, apparently. A fiasco.

"In a way, it's even better," Mathilde says after a moment's reflection. "He comes, here, I explain the situation to him calmly, I talk to him about my family problems, your sister, our nephews."

"Our nephews!"

"When you return, he may already be gone."

But Jonathan isn't sure he wants to pass himself off as Mathilde's husband, especially to this – perhaps violent – lover.

"What if he returns tonight to kill me?"

"No, no, of course not."

She gives the hint of a smile. "If he returns, you can hit him with your iron rod ... The baguette on the kitchen counter ... Please, Jonathan."

She seems desperate. He wonders why it's always he who has to pick up the pieces of other people's lives. He shrugs his shoulders. "Fine. I'm leaving."

***

When he returns at two o'clock in the morning, with Florence finally calmed down, at least for the night – he forced her to take two sleeping pills, stayed with her until she fell asleep, and left carrying the pill bottle with him – Jonathan finds the house in darkness. Only a small lamp is lit in the living room. The door to his room is shut. But the sounds coming from it – moaning, sighing, grunting, not to mention the creaking of the box springs – leave no room for doubt. They are screwing in his bed.

Don't be shy, he thinks. Moreover, *Goddess in Gehenna* is on his night table; he can't even work. He sighs. Then he goes into the kitchen, opens the refrigerator door to see if there's any beer left. There isn't. It's shaping up to be a long night. He makes an espresso and goes out to drink it on the deck.

12

Yard Sale on Dante Street

An address on Dante Street follows.
That tree, at the foot of which
Hernando Cortés had cried.
"How about ordering a pizza?" Mathilde suggests.

He's sitting on the steps, surrounded by his stuff. Hasn't sold much today, but it's only the first day. Mustn't get discouraged. Perhaps he didn't put up enough posters in the neighbourhood. And the ones he did put up were not enticing enough. He should have listed what he had to liquidate, described the furniture and items. Eight thirty. Soon the sun will set, but there's still a good hour of daylight. Afterwards, he'll have to start putting away his stuff. Fortunately, the forecast for tomorrow is another sunny day. Rain would be disastrous. People are more likely to buy when the weather is good. They are like the weather: generous when it is – that is, not often – or stingy.

Nothing about the man on his staircase would inspire love, as they say in a song by Aznavour or someone else: early signs of baldness, drooping eyelids, pallid complexion. Thinning light brown hair streaked with grey. As for his build: skinny, but rather tall: It would be noticeable if his shoulders weren't so hunched. He is wearing beige synthetic pants and a pink and grey checked short-sleeved shirt. A watch with a metal band on his left wrist, a silver cross around his neck. Barefoot in his imitation faded leather sandals. Greying toenails – in his case, grey seems to be the dominant colour. What else to say except that his name is Fernand Lespérance – his friends and relatives call him Fern or Ferny – that he celebrated his fiftieth birthday last month and decided it was time for a change of scenery.

As for the stuff scattered around him, well, it's his entire life. He says it himself: "My entire life is here," indicating with an almost timid gesture his odds and ends, then, as if joking: "Goodbye crazy youth," looking, despite everything, a tad melancholy. Because it must not be so easy to separate himself from his past. And even if his youth was not as crazy as all that.

In front of him on the sidewalk, an imitation oak kitchen table with four chairs, one of them missing a rung. On the table, an almost complete set of dishes – eight place settings originally – made in China, a set of glasses, incomplete as well, but in Bohemian crystal, a cut glass salad bowl, a salt and pepper shaker set in the form of elves, a yellow plastic spatula and ladle, two measuring cups, a wicker basket and a breadboard. Knives, forks and assorted spoons in a shoe box.

On the chairs, three dish towels, stained, but clean, a half-dozen napkins and faded floral sheets. All carefully ironed and folded. A few plastic placemats and two wool blankets, one sky blue, the other beige. A shelving unit featuring books – the recipes of Victor Karr, almost new, the complete works of Alphonse Daudet (the bequest of an aunt who was a great reader; he read one of them and stopped there), about twenty dog-eared detective novels (those have been read several times), *How to Succeed in Business, Feel Good about Yourself and Enjoy Life, the Crossword Dictionary* – DVDs and CDs – including all by Paolina Sanchez, prima donna of tango – a pile of various magazine from the last ten years – there are collectors for that as for everything else. Especially as some of the magazines have long been out of print. Another shelving unit, chipped metal, this time.

On one shelf, a toaster and a coffee maker; on another, an old cassette radio and an iron; on a third, a DVD player with a year's warranty left. A coffee table strewn with knick-knacks, a ceramic vase – the work of a Quebec craftsman – an alarm clock, a cup featuring the words *Geminis are geniuses* – his birthday falls on the first day of the sign – filled with pens and pencils. Pots and pans in cardboard boxes. A few games – checkers, chess, backgammon, Clue and Monopoly. He found the game of Clue covered in dust on the high shelf in his bedroom closet. He didn't know he still had it. He used to play it to entertain Cynthia when she was little; he had custody every other weekend. A large ashtray on a stand.

In fact, he now lights a cigarette, a no-name, Native, that they sell in plastic bags. His delivery man brings him two of them every Saturday morning. He transfers them to old packages of John Player Special – that was the brand he smoked when he could afford it. "Times are hard," he mutters. "But it will change. It will change." When he sells everything, which shouldn't take much longer. You just have to give these things time. He put up posters – "HUGE LIQ-UIDATION. EVERYTHING MUST BE SOLD" in nearby streets, but not enough. He realizes that now. Because you couldn't say that clients flocked there today.

Tomorrow morning he'll put up some more, farther away. As far as the Jean-Talon Market; there are always so many people there who come from just about everywhere. They may be interested – some prefer things that have a history to new things. Their history gives them value, personality, as it were, a humanity that new things don't have. At least that's what they believe and good for him. Yes, tomor-row morning, very early.

He spent yesterday evening setting the price of each item, noting the numbers in a notebook. Everything ends in 99, taxes included – this piece of information written in red on a piece of cardboard placed prominently on the table, even if Cynthia repeated to him at least three times that you never add tax in a garage sale. But he insists. "It's a strong incentive in sales," he answered her. "Customers are more inclined to buy when there's no tax." She rolled her eyes.

Dishtowels: three for $1.99. Set of glasses: $19.99. Same price for the set of dishes. DVDs: $4.99 each. A question of psychology: It's not for nothing that he spent the last thirty years selling in stores. Furniture, sporting goods, hardware, shoes, no matter what. Guinea pigs, snakes, mice – his most recent job was in a pet shop. Ninety-nine is the magic number. Yes, thirty years in sales. But that's over.

On the step beside him, a tin of coffee filled with pennies for making change. An assortment of plastic grocery bags. Now the stores sell them. He'll provide them for free.

The rest – almost new household appliances ($399.99 each, $999.99 for the set of three), bedroom furniture ($499.99, mattress in good condition included), mahogany dining room set: table and five chairs (Cynthia took the sixth to furnish what she calls her office; he wonders what she does aside from chatting on Facebook with her three hundred and fifty-five friends), a sideboard ($1999.99, cannot be sold separately), a hide-a-bed, a TV – the rest is in the unit, four and a half rooms, an upper duplex facing the park, on Dante Street in Little Italy.

"Yes, my entire life," he thinks again. "Well, half, if I make it to one hundred. Let's say two thirds. Mustn't become attached." The salad bowl was a wedding gift from he can't remember who. His wife left it to him when she took off, ten years ago, when they split up their goods – a vile, even sordid task, he remembers. But she took the matching candlesticks, the fondue pot and forks. The couple of elves, one blue (the female) with a red hat, her red comrade with the blue hat, were given to him by his daughter Cynthia on his fortieth birthday; he had just separated. Sentimental value. He didn't set a price. He'll take what he is offered. But no, come to think of it, he won't sell them, he'll take them with him instead. He removes them from the table, places them in a bag so that no possible buyer will be tempted.

Cynthia claims that everything's too expensive, that at those prices he won't sell anything.

"Honestly, Dad, do you really think anyone is going to buy your old dishtowels? Even I wouldn't take them. And five dollars for a DVD when you can download all the movies you want for free."

What does she mean, for free? Pirating? She shrugged her shoulders. Anyway, he'll see. He thinks he can always lower the prices; he's not against the idea of bargaining. But at the last minute, not before.

He calmly smokes his cigarette, stubs it out in a chipped saucer – no chance of selling it, might as well use it as an ashtray. He kept a few pieces of unmatched dishes, a skillet, a beat-up saucepan. You have to still live after all, while you wait.

At nine fifteen, company arrives. Raoul Potvin, his neighbour since he moved here – ten years ago – has just parked his taxi in front of the house. "Do you have time for a beer?" Fernand says, seeing him arrive. They are both now sitting on the staircase, a can in hand.

"Heck of a nice day."

Fernand nods his head and takes a sip.

"The spring was awful, but it looks like we're going to have a summer."

"I hope so for you," Fernand says. "For me, it will be winter when I get there."

He's going to Argentina.

"It's the opposite of us. But they don't have snow like here. Even in winter you can eat outdoors in Buenos Aires, they say. I'm done with shovelling."

Raoul lights a cigarette – not a Native one – and offers him the package. Fernand accepts gratefully: It's not every day he has a chance to smoke a real one. They smoke in silence for a few moments. A grey cat – or is it Dama, the lost cat whose photo stands alongside that of Loulou the parrot on trees in the neighbourhood? – crosses the street in a flash before disappearing in the half-light of Dante Park.

"So," Raoul says, "are you happy with the way the sale's going?"

"More or less. I just sold the salad bowl not five minutes ago. I didn't get my asking price, but I sold it. That's what counts."

"As you say."

"Aside from that, some stuff, two or three DVDs and my crossword dictionary. There's a girl who's going to take the bookshelves. She's supposed to come pick them up tomorrow. Then a couple is going to call me back for the appliances. They offered me five hundred for all three. I said I'd think about it, but I think I'll agree."

"Seems reasonable to me," Raoul says. "I thought you were asking a bit much for used stuff."

"Better to start off high and reach a fair price. Though I think offering five hundred is a bit of nerve, don't you? I haven't even had them a year. Of course, I didn't plan on giving up my place when I bought them. I haven't even finished paying for them. Anyway, they understood that I was in a hurry to get rid of them. Some people always try to take advantage of any opportunity … By the way, do you need anything? I'd make you a good price."

"I have other things on my mind right now," Raoul replies. "I'll take a look at what's left tomorrow."

"There may not be anything left."

"I'd be surprised."

In fact, he doesn't need anything. And other people's old stuff is not his thing.

Three giggling teenagers stop in front of the display. Two of them examine the CDs and DVDs; the third handles the crystal glasses. "Careful not to break anything!" Fernand shouts. They leave without saying goodbye, not buying anything. After shifting everything. Fernand sighs noisily.

Raoul finishes his beer, sets the can down on the step. "I don't know about you, but I'm starving," he says. "What about a pizza?" He gestures to the Trattoria Da Luciano a little farther down the street. One of the most popular restaurants in the neighbourhood, always packed. Right now, about fifteen people are standing about in front of the entrance, waiting for tables to become available. "I'll buy if you give me another beer."

Fernand is surprised. "You haven't eaten yet? I thought you usually had dinner at the End of the World before starting your evening."

"I haven't eaten."

He says it in a strange, tight voice. "So did you decide? Yes or no for the pizza?"

"I thought I'd take in my things before night-time, but a pizza from chez Da Luciano is not to be refused."

While Raoul heads over to the pizzeria, Fernand takes out two placemats from the pile of linens and goes to find two cold beers in the fridge. He pushes away the knick-knacks on the table, takes two plates and collects knives and forks from the shoe box. Then a woman stops in front of the books, leafs through them and offers five dollars for the lot of detective novels. Fernand has trouble concealing his disappointment. He was expecting at least double that, but doesn't feel like haggling, especially as Raoul is now exiting the pizzeria, a large box under his arm.

"I forgot to ask what kind you liked, so I got an all dressed," Raoul says, returning. "Without anchovies."

"You were right, that's the best ... By the way, Argentina won."

"Won what?"

He almost roared. It's the word "won" that he can't swallow.

"The game," Fernand says, nonplussed. "The soccer game. The World Cup, don't you know? Argentina won against Bulgaria."

Raoul shrugs his shoulders.

"I couldn't watch it, obviously, but a guy told me the score earlier. The one who may buy my appliances. Two nothing for Argentina. I was happy."

They sit down at the table on the sidewalk and take two slices of pizza from the box. The first bites are eaten without talking, then Raoul clears his throat, as if preparing to make an important announcement.

"You'll tell me it's none of my business," he says, "but I wonder if you're not getting a little depressed."

Fernand almost chokes. "Why do you say that?"

"It seems to me you decided this very suddenly. It's not natural."

"It seems sudden, but I've been thinking about it for a long time. It was just that I didn't talk about it. Call it a childhood dream."

Raoul nods his head, chewing on another mouthful. "It isn't natural," he says again.

Fernand scowls and Raoul understands that he'd better change the topic. This whole business is none of his business. Besides, Fernand is not a close friend, just a neighbour. He doesn't have any close friends. But he can't stop himself. And talking about the other guy's problems is a way to avoid thinking about the incident. Everything that happened in the restaurant earlier that evening. He doesn't want to think about it. He burned his bridges, he knows. Never will he be brave enough to return there. He'd almost made a family for himself at the End of the

World, with Diderot, Marjolaine and the others. And they were on the verge of starting up their evening card games again.

"You wouldn't be the first, Fern," he says. "You don't have to be ashamed to confide in someone. Psychologists call it a mid-life crisis. Didn't you just turn fifty?"

"So?"

"I was just wondering if you shouldn't see someone."

Fernand lets his fork fall on the table.

"Just because a person changes his life doesn't mean he's crazy," he says. "There's no reason for life not to change. There's no reason for us to always live the same lives. The same damned life till the end."

"I didn't say that, Ferny. Changing your life I can understand. I sometimes even think of doing it myself. Don't you think I'm fed up with mine, sometimes? Do you think I don't miss my Francine?"

These last words are said in a low voice. Raoul has been an inconsolable widower for two years. His wife died of a degenerative disease with an unpronounceable name. She'd had it for a long time. A woman who always smiled despite her suffering. Fernand remembers: She was almost a saint, and far too nice for a surly guy like Raoul Potvin; on that, everyone agreed without saying it aloud.

Raoul shakes his head. "I understand a person wants to go away. But Argentina … you have to admit it's not next door."

"Exactly."

"To tell the truth, I'm afraid that you've started an Internet affair."

"What Internet affair?"

"Don't play innocent, Ferny. You know what I'm talking about. Dating sites. You chat, like they say, with people you've never seen. You fall in love with a photo, then when you finally meet up with the person in the flesh they don't look anything like it. It's not the same person. There are tons of people who are taken in by that type of racket. That's not your case, I hope?"

"Come on. Do I look to you like the type of guy to become infatuated with a photo?"

"It's happened to others."

"Stop worrying, Raoul. The person who's going to take me in has not been born yet."

But Raoul does not seem convinced. "You're not going to have me believe there's not something fishy going on. And usually in this type of affair, it comes down to a woman."

"You know I don't need to go all the way to Argentina to find a woman."

Which is far from being true. Since his separation ten years ago, it can't be said that he's had much success in love. What is true, however – though he doesn't talk of it as no one would understand – is that he has been taking tango lessons for a year at the Porteño Academy. Even Cynthia doesn't know. But that's how he got the idea. Then, little by little, it germinated. He's no longer the same man when he goes there. No more hunched shoulders; he dances with a straight back, careful of his steps. The teacher assures him he has talent.

He's heard of mythical milongas in Buenos Aires: La Confitería Ideal, El Beso and La Maldita, where women always outnumber the men and never refuse to dance. You don't even have to buy them a drink. All they ask is that you dance with them. Some milongas are open in the afternoon; others are open all night. And life over there is quite a bit less expensive than here. You rent a room, a large room in a house where you can cook in a communal kitchen. With his savings and the profits from the garage sale, he could live for at least a year if he's careful. He'll take advantage of it to learn Spanish. Afterwards, he's bound to find something. Perhaps even a woman who'll call him Fernando. He has always gotten by. He knows how to do everything: painting, drywalling and carpentry. He can do plumbing and electrical repairs. Little jobs are always available.

"Besides, I don't even have Internet at home," he says, as if there could be no comeback to that.

Raoul doesn't reply. He takes a swig of beer, removes the last two slices of pizza from the box.

"What you don't understand," Fernand says, "is the time of everyone staying in their own little village until the end of their days is through. This is the era of globalization; now everyone is on the move. There are more Latinos than pure laine Québécois in the neighbourhood, have you noticed? If they have the right to live here, I don't see why we aren't entitled to live among them as well. There's the country where you are born, that you don't choose. Then there's the one that you choose. That one is your true country. I've made my choice. Argentina."

"If you see it like that," Raoul says.

"If you wait too long, it's too late. You're not going to start a new life when you're seventy-five."

"Maybe you're right."

"If I stayed all these years, it was for Cynthia. She doesn't need me anymore."

Raoul says nothing. He has two children, and two grandchildren, and doesn't see them very often. Christmas, Easter, birthdays – and not all: That's what their family get-togethers amount to now. And this year, they all forgot Father's Day. Not even a phone call. Not that he places much importance on it. No. He's always claimed that those holidays were Hallmark holidays, forcing people to spend money. Yet this year he would have appreciated a word, a card, an invitation from one or the other, something to say they remembered he existed. A matter of principle. True, they don't have the same schedules: They work during the day and he works nights and weekends.

In Francine's day, it was different. They would see each other every Sunday at lunch. For her that get-together was sacred. She would have reminded them about Father's Day and there would have been a cake (bought at a bakery, she no longer had the strength to cook) and presents, even symbolic ones. All those ties that he never wore.

"It's like with family," Fernand is now saying, not short on comparisons. "You don't choose your parents or your children. Your friends, yes. Your friends are your real family. In your case, there are the ones you play cards with, for example …"

"Change the subject!" Raoul says, cutting him short.

They've finished the pizza. Almost eleven o'clock; night has definitively fallen. At the trattoria, all the customers from the line up have now entered. The grey cat leaves the park, crosses the street and goes to hide beneath the taxi.

Fernand thinks it's high time he takes in his things, but Raoul seems to want to linger. That isn't like him. Usually, at this hour, he's been driving in the city for a long time. Since Francine died, he's been working at night. Says it's not as hard during the day to sleep all alone in his bed. With all his speeches on the mid-life crisis at fifty earlier, he may have really been talking about himself. As they say, it's easier to criticize the faults of others than to recognize your own. In love with a photo, probably not, but on the verge of depression ... Fernand wouldn't be surprised. He is working too much, not eating right – always in restaurants – drinking too much beer, smoking like a chimney. He's the one who should see someone.

He could ask Raoul to help him, to carry the table at least. Strange that he does not offer. This morning, Cynthia gave him a hand. He won't be able to manage alone. And if he puts it underneath the staircase, it's liable to be stolen.

"Would you like a coffee?" he asks. "My coffeemaker is for sale, but I can make us instant."

"Instant – not really. But I'd gladly take another beer."

"Will you be OK to drive?"

"Forget it if you don't want to. I'll go get another one at my place."

"Don't get mad."

There were two left. Fernand set them on the table. He made coffee for himself. All of a sudden he's tired. He's been there since eight o'clock this morning. And tomorrow, he has another big day ahead of him. He'd planned to get up at dawn to put up some posters. And the other one is lingering, as if planning to spend the night. Fernand wishes he'd go to work, or go home, which would probably be better given his condition. Impaired, as they say. If he had an accident, even a collision, he'd lose his licence. He lights a Native cigarette.

But Raoul raises the issue again.

"There's another thing that grates on me," he says – his speech is now slurred. "You're getting rid of all your things, just like that. What if you don't like it over there in Argentina and decide to come back here. You're going to find yourself with nothing, in the lurch."

"No danger of that. No chance that I won't like it."

"You're really keeping nothing?"

"My clothes, obviously. And a few photos. I don't need much. My razor, my toothbrush. I want to start new, not weigh myself down with memories. Just this."

He takes the two elves out of the plastic bag. "A gift from Cynthia."

Raoul takes the last sip of his beer.

"Well, that's it, Fernand, my friend. I'm going to have to think about getting to work. Got to keep the wolf from the door."

He gets up heavily – as if his own weight had suddenly become too heavy for him – staggers toward his taxi parked in front.

"And thanks for the beer."

"No problem, Raoul. Any time. Especially as I won't be here much longer."

Then, at the moment Raoul arrives at the car, Fernand cries out: "Careful. I think there's a cat beneath your car."

But Raoul doesn't open the door.

"You know what? I envy you for being able to leave."

He doesn't say anything else, just leans back against the elm in front of the house.

"You don't really seem yourself," Fernand says, alarmed. "I think you'd be better off going to bed tonight."

Raoul says nothing. Then he explodes, but in a voice that is almost low: Fernand has to draw near.

"This evening I did something I regret. Yes, I damn well regret it, I'll tell you. But it's too late. You can't go back. One thing that I know is I can never repair what I did. I'll never be able to forgive myself for it."

Then a strange noise. As if he is crying. Yes, leaning back against the elm, he suddenly heaves big sobs, his face in his hands.

About the Author

Hélène Rioux has published poetry, short stories, translations, and ten novels. She received the Prix France-Québec and the Prix Ringuet de l'Académie des Lettres du Québec for *Mercredi soir au Bout du monde* (translated by Jonathan Kaplansky as *Wednesday Night at the End of the World*), the *Grand Prix littéraire du Journal de Montréal,* and the Prix de la Société des Écrivains canadiens for *Chambre avec baignoire.* She has been a finalist for the Governor General's Literary Award six times. She has also translated into French books by Elizabeth Hay, Yann Martel, Jeffrey Moore, and Johanna Skibsrud. Her novels have been translated into English, Spanish, and Bulgarian.

About the Translator

Jonathan Kaplansky's translations include *Things Seen* by Annie Ernaux, *Days of Sand* by Hélène Dorion, *Frank Borzage: The Life and Films of a Hollywood Romantic* by Hervé Dumont, and *The Girl Before, the Girl After* by Louis-Philippe Hébert. He has translated much of Hélène Rioux's fiction, including *Wednesday Night at the End of the World* and *Wandering Souls in Paradise Lost*, and has taught literary translation at the Quebec Writer's Federation. He is a member of the Executive of the Literary Translators' Association of Canada and has served on the juries of the John Glassco Translation Prize and the Governor General's Literary Awards.